LEVELS

KARL FISCHER

Printed in the USA.

ISBN: 978-1-950305-33-9 (sc)
ISBN: 978-1-950305-34-6 (ebook)

First printing edition:
Published by Bizarro Pulp Press in the United States of America.
Cover Design and Layout/Interior Layout Don Noble
Edited by Nicholas Day

Bizarro Pulp Press, an imprint of JournalStone Publishing
3052 Sassafras Trail
Carbondale, Illinois 62901

Bizarro Pulp Press may be ordered through booksellers or by contacting:
JournalStone | www.journalstone.com

For Whitney, the fam, and the friends I left in Portland.
This book is dedicated to my twenties. To a bunch of stupid decisions, as well as all the excellent ones.

Chapter 1—Leonard Gets a Job

Guild Headquarters was a sprawling gothic manor, its glazed bricks the color of dried blood. Thorny spires ensconced the main hall and flying buttresses like spider legs anchored it on the hill's precarious summit. Spread below was downtown Castaway, where ancient stone rowhouses formed a hedge of village squalor around Central Plaza. Here, the exotic and varied items of value found across the Levels could be exchanged for any sordid, godless thing an adventurer might want.

Smoke shops, apothecaries, soothsayers, arsenals, bars, bistros, bordellos, casinos, outlet stores, and more. Working-class Municipals made their money here, as did the retired adventurers who couldn't hack it on the Levels anymore. Central Plaza was also the Elevator's terminus. Dozens of guards were stationed here. All Munis—not a Castaway among them—decked out in cybernetic body armor equipped with shoulder-mounted rockets, hyperion lasers, and other futuristic-nonsense weaponry. They scanned everyone who went in and out.

Just to the left of the Elevator was our one-way portal, a mysterious and ancient dimensional anomaly that would spit up three or four lost souls a day. This kept our population steady. Supposedly, the portal used to go both ways, and people moved freely between Castaway, the Levels, and the rest of the Multiverse, but I wasn't around for that.

"Welcome to Castaway!" we'd all shout when a terrified individual came tobogganing out of the Æther, often covered in blood, sometimes clutching the empty air where they might have embraced a loved one just moments before.

No one was clear on the rules for getting portaled to Castaway because no one could remember their lives before they arrived. We had many rules about how to treat new arrivals, with the most important being to greet them warmly and sincerely, no matter how shitty of a day you were having.

"I need to get back," a new arrival screamed. "I need to get home. Please, for the love of God, send me back!"

"You're in shock," said a Guild escort, flanked by several Muni guards. "You've been brought to Castaway."

"She's dying! Why won't anyone help me?"

"Just come with us, sir, and all will be explained."

"Welcome to Castaway," I told the tear-streaked individual as he was led off. "Keep your chin up, pal. It gets easier."

After the fall of Intergalactic Automated Luxury Communism came the Loot Rush of PY 0xC35A. Boom towns sprang up like weeds, the first of which was our very own Castaway. Settlers were more concerned with turning a profit than slaying evil, leaving entities like the Shrike King and the Haver-of-Faces alone to rule their dark kingdoms. The so-called Easy Levels, like The Goblin Warrens and The House of Mummies, were converted into loot farms. Tedious as hell.

With limitless wealth and fantastical weaponry at their disposal, the Loot Rush-era nutjobs took things a step further by establishing their own nation state, barring all other transdimensional governments from sending "privateers" to pillage their sovereign territory. Thus began the Hero Wars, a period of history subject to such embellishment and outright fabrication that a coherent narrative could never be established, not even amongst its veterans.

The repercussions, however, were clear enough.

With the rogue nation state dismantled and its leaders executed, the Adventurer's Guild was established to prevent future generations of treasure-hunting lunatics from attaining the loftiest heights of wealth ever again. The Guild became one of the Multiverse's largest publicly-traded superpowers, and many years later, I made the idiotic decision to join them.

My palms were sweaty and sensitive. Why was I so nervous?

The mansion's doors opened automatically for me, leading to a foyer awash in the excess of our Guild dues. Vaulted ceilings encompassed a grand ballroom, the floors and molding crafted from rarest hardwoods, the walls lined with candelabras of gold and Argot crystal. Stained glass windows filtered the sunlight, lending heavy, incandescent colors to the perfumed air. A sign directed me down a hallway of mounted heads, each a bestial horror from distant lands, to a waiting room filled with plastic chairs.

A stuffed griffin held a ticket dispenser in its beak.

It gave me number ninety-eight.

There were a few end tables stacked with magazines like *Paladin Monthly* and its somewhat raunchier cousin *Soldier of Loot.* A moderate crowd had queued up for interviews—Debra Canes, Horace Wilks, Ebenezer von Dread, Laura Bosco, Knives Conrad, and the Mighty Minotaur, to name a few. Some had been on quests with me. Some were my neighbors.

We all smiled at each other like comrades, but familiarity was not closeness.

Sometimes, I would get the idea in my head to throw a party and invite everyone in Castaway. Just go nuts. Fuck this bullshit career and have some fun before we all died. The feeling dissipated as soon as it arrived.

Folks were hard to impress around here. Survival, though rare, held little clout. We remembered each other fondly of course—each stupid, expendable face—but something pressed on our emotions, truncating them, compacting us into creatures that were small and disposable. Here one day and gone the next. It was exhausting to care overly much.

A squad of folks in identical, beetle black, full body armor trooped into the waiting room. They had serious guns, all matching, and a serious stride. Their faces were obscured. They were obviously not from Castaway.

I nodded at them. None of them nodded back.

"Hey, Mr. Marcs!"

I smelled him before I saw him.

Dead Tomas stumbled into my life, into my field of vision, into the chair opposite me.

Tomas was once a normal reanimated corpse soldier—a standard Warrior Melee Zombie—but after going to the Blight Level without protective gear, his flesh became a walking mass of tumors that constantly underwent cellular differentiation, producing hair and teeth and organs that were shed across town. Worse yet, a demon gestated inside him. It would eventually chew its way out and start a rampage. Demons couldn't breathe Level 1's purified air, but even in the throes of death, they could do a lot of damage.

Dead Tomas smiled his disease-ridden smile. "You never call me. And you don't come around to the mall neither. What's up with that?"

"I've been busy," I said.

"You were on assignment?"

"Little projects, you know?"

"Oh, I know what you mean." Dead Tomas reclined heavily on the cheap folding chair, his bulk dripping over the sides. "Last week, I started writing. Poetry, mostly, but I guess they're more like song lyrics. Can you believe that?"

"Should I not?"

"I never thought I was the creative type, but maybe I have the pieces of a songwriter in me. I'm thinking of taking up an instrument. Imagine if I was good enough to switch Designation. A Zombie Bard."

The PA called up number thirty-eight. No one stood.

"So…" Dead Tomas let the word hang between us, a string of linguistic mucous from which I could not detach myself. "You doing anything later?"

In a perfect world, coercive questions such as these would be illegal without a notarized Writ of Friendship. But in our horrible world of ambiguity and expectations, no polite method existed for me to reasonably avoid saying what I was about to say.

"Shifty Eyes Frank is coming back tonight. We're partying at The Lounge."

Dead Tomas looked like a kid in a candy store. "Room for one more?"

"Easily." I hated myself. "We start at 7 o'clock."

"Man, I haven't been to The Lounge in ages. Usually, if I drink, I just go to the Darkness on the Edge of Town. It's amazing how many bars Castaway has. I guess that's what happens when an adventurer lives long enough to retire."

We lapsed into silence. It could have been a comfortable one. A natural respite from the conversation.

My mouth betrayed me again.

"I always wanted to own my own place," I said. "Like a billiard parlor. Or maybe a dive bar with cheap, terrible drinks. And arcade games. Retro pinball machines and the like."

Dead Tomas leaned in. "What would you call it?"

"I don't know. Probably Lenny's Place."

"Seems plain."

"The name wouldn't matter. It would be in a safe zone on top of a mountain or something. A tiny vestige of civilization."

Dead Tomas stroked his bulbous chin. "You'd need a gimmick to stand out. You could serve ice cream. If I went to a bar that had ice cream, I would never go anywhere else."

I almost slapped myself. Why was I spilling my guts to Dead Tomas of all people? He'd done more than coerce me into inviting him out. Now he was forcing me to socialize in a waiting room. We were making a connection.

This madness had to stop.

The PA called up number one oh five.

"That's me!" Dead Tomas rose, leaving behind an assortment of oozes in the chair. "Good luck, Leonard! Maybe we'll get the same quest."

I waved him off. How did he get ahead of me in line?

The PA continued to call up random numbers. Those of us stuck in purgatory were whittled away until it was just me and the guys in identical black armor.

None of them had tickets.

I couldn't be sure if they were looking at me or not.

"Number ninety-eight. Now helping number ninety-eight."

I bolted for the front desk.

The clerk directed me down a colonnade to the great hall. Beneath the rich mosaics of the clerestory lay a cubicle farm. The sounds of interviews-in-progress reverberated off the tiles, forming a din of eager responses and thoughtful muttering. A hundred psychological experiments conducted at once.

The desperation was palpable.

Another clerk brought me to an empty cubicle and told me to wait.

In the good old days—the days on which I cut my teeth—a support guy wrote his own ticket, even with a niche Designation like mine. Castaway once had a glut of violent bruisers. Good at slaying monsters but little else. This was what we called the Whoopass Metric, and whoopass was only as good as the finesse that guided it. Then came the Massacre on Level 13, a botched attempt at slaying Bob Alpha, possibly the toughest opponent the Levels had to offer. Whoever commissioned it knew nothing about team composition and had stacked the party with every meathead they could buy. Too much whoopass. Not enough finesse. The result was an unmitigated shitshow. No loot, and no survivors except the legendary Wolfram Selma.

Since then, Castaway experienced a perennial shortage of good muscle. Even with an uptick in portaled newcomers, the industry had yet to recover. It's why Shifty Eyes Frank was coming home with a mountain of gold and I was going down to Guild Headquarters with my hat in hand.

"Hello," said my interviewer, arriving loudly. "How are we today, Mr. Marcs?"

She had big round eyes and an inviting face; her features soft but articulated. Dark hair in a carefree bob. Much cuter than any placement officer I had ever seen before. Not a former adventurer either. Was she new in town? Her nametag read "Anita M." in Clerical General, a dialect of the Universal script that most people could not read. They did it on purpose to intimidate.

She noticed me reading her nametag and made a note on her clipboard. "How are we today? You didn't answer my question."

"We? I don't know. Myself, I'm doing okay. What about you?"

"It's a figure of speech, Mr. Marcs. I didn't actually think you knew how I was doing. And as much as I appreciate the question—because I'm not doing well at all, you see, I have these headaches, and so much more—I am the interviewer here, not you. You need to leave the question-asking to me. They pay me big bucks to ask questions. Do you think that's fair?"

"Yes, Anita. That's entirely fair and I'm happy you asked me if it was fair. It shows you have respect for my feelings and it makes me want to reciprocate that level of respect."

"Yes, yes." Anita appeared to be writing down my words verbatim. "But please call me misses, uh, Miss Menard."

"I didn't know that was your name."

"It says so right on my nametag."

"It says 'Anita M.' on your nametag."

She grimaced. "Well, my name is Anita Menard. That's what the 'M' stands for, and nothing else. You and I don't know each other well enough for you to call me Anita. Or sweetie. Or sugar tits."

"I would never call you those things," I said.

"You might," she replied, somewhat defensively, "if we were in a relationship. But you're right, it would be highly inappropriate otherwise. Does that make sense to you?"

"It makes a lot of sense, Ms. Menard, and I'm really glad you asked that question, because I've always felt that my greatest accomplishment has been learning to accept change and take responsibility for my actions."

Her eyes widened. "You don't say."

"I do say, Ms. Menard. Some people tell me that I'm almost too good at interpersonal communication, which is why I feel that I would be a huge asset on this mission."

Her eyes shrunk back down. "I haven't mentioned any mission."

Shit, I was getting ahead of myself.

She took more notes. "Mr. Marcs, please use exactly five words to describe how you would contribute to the success of any hypothetical mission, regardless of what Level it's on. Infer nothing."

"Poise, stamina, interpersonal communication, and tenacity."

"That's six words."

"You counted 'and?' That's just an article."

"Articles count." Anita paused in her notetaking. "Everything counts."

I slid in my chair.

"Can you neutralize an adult humanoid with your bare hands?"

"No, ma'am, not at this time."

"I see. And can you hit a moving target with a projectile weapon from a distance of fifty yards or greater?"

"No, ma'am, not at this time."

"How about a knot in a cherry stem? Can you tie one off with your tongue?"

"Yes, ma'am. Yes, I could."

"And why do you feel that you would be a good fit for this hypothetical mission, of which you know nothing and have inferred nothing because I haven't told you anything about it?"

"I'm an independent thinker, Ms. Menard. I follow instructions, but I always take risks, without endangering the enterprise. Where I excel most is employing bold, novel strategies that ensure consistent results easily measured by the latest KPIs."

Anita nodded serenely. "Yes. These are the things I'm told that I want to hear. We really need someone who can think outside the box on this one. Not just someone who knows how to follow, but someone who knows how to lead. Someone who knows how to follow the process and get the job done. A real team player, if you will."

"I am nothing if not a team player."

"Horse crap. You're a man on the edge, Leonard Marcs. I know your type. This is where I would normally ask how you could improve your performance, but I'd like to try something different with you. We're testing an experimental HR process. Do you mind?"

"Not at all, Ms. Menard."

"Goodie. I'm going to read a list of words and phrases. With each item, I want you to say the first word that comes to mind. Just one word. No more. No less. Do you understand what I'm asking, Mr. Marcs?"

"I do and I'm very glad you asked if I understood, Ms. Menard."

"I'm glad that you're glad, Mr. Marcs."

"I'm glad that you're glad, Ms. Menard, and I look forward to speaking with you more about this opportunity."

"You are a delight. Are you ready? Here we go…"

Apple

"Pie."

Sword

"Whoopass."

Gangrenous

"Toe."

Adventurer's Guild

"Profitable."

Lovers entwined, two hearts enshrined, I bite your butt.

"…inappropriate?"

You're no fun. What about the name El Savel?

"Who?"

I'm asking the questions, Mr. Marcs. Please don't interrupt.

"Sorry."

The Lathes of Heaven

"Uh…"

The Ninth Lathe of Heaven, called Facilitator

"I got nothing."

Anita snapped her pen in half. "Are you incapable of following even the simplest instruction? One word. One. You gave me three."

"Ms. Menard—"

"You're an empty-headed little pawn, aren't you, Leonard Marcs?"

Things were getting oddly personal. Was this part of the interview?

Anita took a deep breath and reviewed her notes. "You scored very well on that test. I do believe I have a commission available."

"Really?" I could hardly believe my luck. "Thank you, Ms. Menard."

"The only complication is that your party is scheduled to arrive on Level 2 in about twenty minutes. I apologize for the short notice. We had a cancellation."

I was starting to believe my luck again. "Level 2? That's the Corporate Level. That's for greenhorns."

"Admittedly, you are overqualified," she said languidly, "but it's all I have. Your quest is simple enough. Shouldn't take more than seven or eight hours. Would you like to hear the details?"

"I guess."

"The once-peaceful and verdant LLC of Axiom Data Products has been overrun by a fearsome menace: *sloppy workload management.* Their databases are considerably out-of-date, and it's the end of the quarter! The only way to save regional leadership is to really knuckle down, pump up the jams, and do some data entry. 50 WPM or more. Will you accept this quest, Leonard Marcs?"

I sighed long and loud. "How much does it pay?"

"Eight funbucks an hour. And free bagels on Tuesdays."

"It's not Tuesday."

Anita shuffled some papers. "Well, if you're available next Tuesday, I can get you the same quest. In fact, this could be a regular job."

"Once is enough for now."

She flipped open a manila folder that had my name on it. "Are you sure? Your record is full of gaps. Your numbers aren't great either. Level 2 may not be glamorous, but it's steady. Could really put the wind back in your sails."

I glowered at her. "Let me ask you something, Anita—"

"Mrs. Menard. Or rather, Ms. Menard, please."

"Person to person, Ms. Anita Menard. Is this enough for you? This life. Does it satisfy you? I mean, we're working for the Adventurer's Guild. We're supposed to be heroes. This is more like a glorified temp agency. I don't know what they're paying you, but eight funbucks an hour ain't shit for me. I got skills! What about you? Is this meaningful enough for you?"

Anita leaned forward and really looked at me for the first time, the full effect of her undivided attention devastating. "What's meaning got to do with it, Lenny? Someone wants a basilisk slain. Someone else wants their database updated. I don't give a shit. I do this job because it gives me something I want. It's an exchange."

"And that makes you happy?" I asked.

She gazed at me quite sadly. "It will in time. But it's my choice. You have to choose these things—they don't just happen. I can't give you a job that'll make you happy, Leonard. Only you can make you happy."

The acrylic throw rugs that decorated Anita's cubicle looked cheap and garish on top of the rich, antique parquet.

"Alright," I said, "I'll take the job."

Chapter 2—Leonard and the Gang Unwind

After clearing out my docket, I spent my last hour at Axiom Data Products breaking goblin charges with a stapler. Goblins were quite small and did not like being stapled in the forehead.

The Corporate Level, formerly known as The Goblin Warrens, consisted of many hundreds of tunnels and subterranean rooms filled to bursting with modular workstations, ergonomic furniture, and other future-forward office solutions. Many features of the Level's original motif—a classic hack-and-slash affair combined with simple puzzle mechanics and hidden booby traps—were preserved in the slatted walls and rough-hewn stone archways that adorned the break rooms.

Goblins were not difficult to kill, and in fact, it was better to leave them un-killed so they might accumulate more loot in the deepest tunnels where they dwelt. Plus, older goblins were even easier to overcome than spryer, younger goblins full of hope and dignity. Goblin loot was poor in quality but reliably plentiful, and since their attacks were both predictable and easily-defeated, enterprising corporations figured, "Why not do some extra work while you wait for the next invasion?"

Before leaving the Corporate Level, I stopped at their 7-Eleven for a cup of coffee. I didn't need more coffee—I'd been drinking coffee all day and more coffee would make me want to kill myself—but drinking with Shifty Eyes later would offset the caffeine.

Today was a day for getting fucked up.

The Corporate Level 7-Eleven was one of the better-stocked franchise locations I had ever patronized, offering a wide array of coffees: Shrike King Medium, Galactic Bold, Houndstooth, Flight-o-Doves, Murder Junkie, and something called Hazelnut. I poured the usual fifty-two ounces of Galactic Bold, black, no sugar, and just a dab of psilocybin. The clerk didn't even seem to mind that I muttered to myself.

"How's your day going?" the clerk asked in a tinny voice, his jaw out-of-sync with his words.

I inspected him. "Didn't they program you not to end your sentences with prepositional phrases?"

"TGIF!"

"Why? Don't you work every day?"

The clerk raised his arm in a gesture that was either a wave or the start of a high-five. "Living the dream, buddy."

There were mini taco-dogs on the roller. I only had a stale bagel for lunch.

The clerk tracked my wistful gaze. "Two for a 'buck!"

"A what?"

"Just one funbuck!"

"That's what I thought you meant."

I asked for four taco-dogs and handed the clerk an amethyst shard.

"We don't accept stones," the clerk replied with a different, more assertive voice. "Cash only."

Sighing loudly, I traded him a low-denomination of fiat money. That's when I noticed the guy in the alligator costume.

It was a cheesy getup, his face poking through the alligator's mouth. Even hunched over, he was easily six and a half feet tall. Too tall for his own body. He had beady eyes and a patchy curtain of facial hair. I might not have noticed him. But he drank his slushie at an incredible volume, and gave me the hairy eyeball while he did it. His eyes burned like a laser in my brain.

"Who the hell is that?" I asked the clerk.

"Here's your change, sir," the clerk replied, dumping coins on the floor.

"How long's he been loitering there?"

"Have a pleasant day, sir."

"What's your name? I want to speak to your manager."

The clerk was out of lines to say.

I turned to the Alligator Man. "You got a problem, pal?"

The Alligator Man drained his slushie. "Suppose I did." He went to the machine and got a refill. "You gonna do something about it?"

I tried to fume at him menacingly.

The Alligator Man took a huge gulp of blue raspberry and exhaled loudly."Don't you ignore me," I told him.

"I'm not," he said. "I'm looking right at you."

"Listen, buddy." I fought for something bold to say. "One day you're gonna piss off the wrong guy with that."

The Alligator Man smacked his lips. "Does that make you the right guy?"

I didn't have a retort.

"Go home, Leonard Marcs." He said my name with perfect familiarity.

I was so mad at the Alligator Man for being tougher and more mysterious that I left without my taco-dogs.

—

Packed into the Elevator, we descended from the sky-ceiling over Castaway and passed through the heart of her larger sister-city, Mezzanine, home to Level 1's Municipal Government. Mezzanine sprouted from the Elevator like a great mushroom cap and we were treated to a cross-sectional view of the floating metropolis as we made our way down. Glittering glass bridges threaded towers of silver crowded with neon lights. Platforms full of inscrutable faces. Munis in line. Munis congregating in malls. Here and there, a Castaway being thrown out of a bar. Dirty sidewalks. Pipes and pilings and septic tanks. The engine house for Mezzanine's anti-gravity system. Open sky again.

Today's sky was a contemplative robin's egg blue. Heavy clouds and lazy, crumbling ziggurats—some of them home to squatters—floated past the Elevator car as we continued our descent, eventually touching down in Central Plaza where dozens of adventurers waited to board.

I felt no small amount of jealousy at the others, who disembarked with bags and backpacks and lunchboxes bursting with dosh, and me with my lousy eight funbucks an hour and this commemorative chicken bucket a goblin had dropped when I stabbed it with a pen. Everything else of value had been surrendered at the Elevator as part of my dues.

The daylight was waning fast but I had some time to kill before The Lounge. I needed a shower, and I couldn't stop fuming about the Alligator Man. What an asshole. How had he known my name? Was I famous? Probably not. Probably some drifter high on mana potions—suffering mild psychic manifestations—wandering the Levels for kicks with no Designation. More common than dirt.

After a swift and angry shit at the Ole Opry Building, which had the best toilets in town, I picked up a bunch of sandwiches at Akk Akk's Deli, downed a quick forty, and headed home.

Castaway wasn't a large town, but its founders had little regard for urban planning. Streets were tangled and few. Most buildings were accessible only by a twisting series of stairs and alleyways. A successful path might involve numerous detours through embowered dells into neighborhoods built like briar patches of jumbled architecture and unmarked entrances. My duplex was no exception. Hidden behind a stand of pine and decorative boulders, it rested halfway up a switchback that climbed to the Fresco District, a quaint marketplace of curio stores and themed bakeries where the Munis would walk around and not buy anything.

Coming up the switchback, I looked for signs of my neighbor Ron. On the one hand, Ron was a good friend and neighbor, and he was still battling depression after losing Howie, so it would be good if he left the house. On the other hand, if Ron was too depressed to go out, that made for a handy excuse to call off the entire evening and avoid Dead Tomas.

To my chagrin, Ron's lights were off.

And someone had knifed a fish to my door.

Was it from Ron?

Whoever it was, they hadn't left a note. No message scrawled in blood.

Just a fish. Knifed to my door.

I waited for someone to jump out of the shadows and deliver a cryptic warning. Or mug me for my sandwiches.

Nothing.

"What's your deal," I asked the fish. "Who put you up to this?"

The fish dripped without comment, slack jawed, indifferent, contemplating the Æther with its glassy, sideways stare. The knife looked expensive. Jewel insets. A long, polished blade, which someone had plunged deep into the fiberboard.

"I will not make time for this," I announced. "If someone wants to threaten me, they can do it properly."

I took a long shower, mutteringly angrily about fish and alligators.

My hands wouldn't stop shaking.

—

The Lounge was my favorite bar. An awful place, but cheap and reliable. All bets were off on Mystery Shot Night. The bartender might piss in a cup and add a jigger of vodka. He might serve you strychnine and fermented apple juice, or mouthwash and ginger kombucha. They once gave me a tall glass of paint thinner and said it was clamato. I still drank it.

I was so jazzed to be getting toasted that I almost forgot how weird the day had been. The past was dead. The future bright.

The Lounge was shoved it into the basement of an oversized office building that no longer had any offices. It used to be a place for Munis until they built Mezzanine. Garish, cornucopia-patterned wallpaper covered the interior, with little in the way of practical furniture. Instead, fainting couches, picnic tables, and wobbly bar stools that were only an ass away from total collapse. The Lounge didn't have a kitchen, but they could microwave a sausage-on-a-stick if you asked. I suspected the owner once managed a bowling alley.

To my surprise, Ron was already here. So was Dead Tomas.

Worse yet, it looked like they were having a good time.

They saw me and waved me over.

Ron had a blonde walrus mustache and a widow's peak so tall he was almost bald. Eyes like storm-drenched skies. Large brands formed patterns of protection across his skin, vital, since he was a Warrior Melee Duelist. The kind of Designation they gave to people who had more skill than sense.

"Leonard!" he shouted with uncharacteristic glee, already deep in his mystery shots. "You didn't tell me DT was gonna be here."

"Me neither," I said, "until I saw him at the Guild this morning."

"You guys must think I'm the busiest zombie in Castaway," said Dead Tomas, knocking back something like curdled milk. "Honestly, I'm always around. We should go to the mall sometime."

"What's with you and the mall?" I demanded.

"Uh, ever heard of soft pretzels? Glow-in-the-dark miniature golf? The best movie theater—not just in Castaway—but anywhere on the Levels? The mall is the shit, my friend."

Barely a minute and I was already annoyed. "They have plenty of movie theaters on Mezz."

"Oh, sure, they've got megaplexes," said Dead Tomas, "but Mezzanine doesn't have a real arthouse theater the way we do."

I rolled my eyes.

"I hate Mezzanine," Dead Tomas continued. "It's over-priced, obnoxious, gentrified, and people treat you like the scum of the Multiverse."

On that I couldn't disagree. Mezzanine was a place of fierce competition and exorbitant housing prices, driven by an economy that made no sense to us adventuring folk. A breeding ground for entitled assholes.

"We need another round," said Ron, hoisting himself off the bench. "What's your poison, Lenny?"

"I'll come with you," I offered.

"Nonsense. Keep DT company. I'll get shots."

They started playing a disco number. I closed my eyes and felt the bassline in my sinuses.

Dead Tomas watched me. "How'd it go?"

"How'd what go?" I asked.

"The interview! What happened? What'd you get?"

"Well," I said, "I went to Level 2 to be a fucking temp. Spent the day correcting spreadsheets, fondling my balls, and warding off goblins with office supplies."

"Oh yeah? That sounds kind of exciting."

"Exciting?" I demanded, mad enough to look him in the eyes.

Dead Tomas shrugged, a little stung. "I don't know. They gave me the Sunken Temple again. No matter what kind of Zombie you are, it's always the environmental obstacles. No one picks you for anything if it isn't walking through gas clouds or searching flooded ruins for keys. So boring!"

It had never occurred to me that Dead Tomas would be relegated to such a pathetic role. Like me, they'd stuck him in a niche. I was powerless to stop the empathy that rose in my chest.

"Say, Tomas…when did you arrive?" I asked.

"About 5:30, I think. I wanted to play pinball."

"That's not what I meant." I took a deep breath. "When did you get to Castaway? When were you portaled here?"

His dead, dishwater eyes got real big. "Hell, I don't know. When did any of us get here? Ten years? Twenty years? More? It's not like we can go back. Honestly, I don't think about it much."

I stared off into the growing crowd, soaking up his words.

"A long time ago," I said, "I went on a mission to Level 21—the Evil Amusement Park Level—and in the haunted funhouse there we found this clock. It was a grandfather clock with beautiful mosaics and big brass hands. We figured it was magic, so we threw it on the cart. And I remember that we were sure it was busted because the hands and the pendulum weren't moving. But days later, when we were humping all our dosh back to the Elevator, I noticed the time had changed. The hands and pendulum had moved ever so slightly. That's when I began to speculate. What if the clock worked? And had shown the correct time all along?"

Dead Tomas scrunched his brow. "If you were jostling it around in the cart, that could have moved the hands."

"Sure. The clock really was broken. But it's what the clock

implied—the idea that none of this is real. What if time is moving differently for us? What if you and I and the Levels are all going at a different speed from the rest of the Multiverse? Or maybe we're perceiving reality at a faster rate. Maybe we think we've been here for decades, but it's only been a few days."

"That's an awful lot of speculation over a busted clock, Leonard."

"There are superluminal particles all around us," I said. "If observed, they would seem to approach and depart at the same time. The Multiverse is built on natural paradoxes. Time is an illusion. There's no telling what's true."

Dead Tomas looked genuinely annoyed, an emotion I had never seen on him before.

"Hey, man, lighten up," I said. "I'm trying to have a real conversation with you for once, instead of…you know."

"No, I don't know. Instead of what?"

I clenched my jaw.

Understanding sunk in and Dead Tomas just stared at his empty shot glasses.

I wanted to feel bad, but felt only embarrassment.

Ron came back with a tray full of juices and cleaning solvents.

He wasn't alone.

Shifty Eyes Frank wasted no time in pulling me off the bench and delivering a hug that nearly broke my ribs. He was built like a bear on steroids, with a massive gut and arms thicker than my head. He also had laterally protruding chameleon eyes that could move independent of each other. They were always looking at other stuff, even when he talked to you.

"Lenny, you weird little bastard!" he crowed, still squeezing me.

I was helpless. I couldn't breathe.

"Part of me was hoping I wouldn't see you," said Shifty Eyes. "Thought maybe you'd get a quest at the last minute. Or maybe meet somebody. Have some fun for once in your miserable life. But hey, I'm here now, so we're gonna party. Holy shit, who invited Dead Tomas?"

Finally released, I caught my breath and explained that I was the one who brought him.

"He felt obligated," Tomas supplied.

Shifty Eyes smirked. "That's because you can't take a hint, zombie boy. You get uglier every time I see you. Look at him and tell me there's a just and omnipotent creator out there in the Multiverse."

Dead Tomas tried to pull his massive legs from underneath the picnic table. "Think I'll go home."

"Hey, don't be like that," said Shifty Eyes. "I'm an asshole. I apologize. Stick around. Let me buy you some drinks. Whaddya say?"

Dead Tomas glanced knowingly at me.

"And Lenny's an asshole too." Shifty Eyes nudged me. "Isn't that right?"

"I'm sorry, Tom," I said, facing him squarely. "I want you to stick around. Please forgive me."

Dead Tomas wiped some bile from the corner of his eye.

"See?" Shifty Eyes clapped me on the back, knocking my teeth together. "That wasn't so terrible. Now let's stop jerking each other off and get toasted, gentlemen. This bag is a supercompressed demi-dimension holding a literal mountain of coins, and I'm gonna make it rain in this bitch."

We began punishing our livers for the sins of our forefathers. We couldn't tell what substances we imbibed, only that they were poisonous and strong. Even as I slipped the bonds of sobriety, I saw our shared desperation for what it was.

The evening passed in a blur of stories and arguments and braggadocio. Often with Shifty Eyes as our catalyst.

"…the Fly Level is no joke, boys. Did you know they taste with their feet? I want you to keep that in mind when I describe to you how Kirkenbach died..."

I never liked Kirkenbach anyway, though I knew that I would feel bad about his death later.

"…and, apparently, it was Red Suzy that knifed Angor. We had Golden Joe figured all wrong! Except for the arson. That was still him…"

The evanescent quality of "having fun" was perpendicular to a serious, goal-oriented state of mind. At the place where the two met was the birth of obsession. A self-perpetuating loop of gratification for the sake of itself.

"...which is why he lost both eyeballs. But, hey, the guy has enough money he can afford new ones. I worry about his dogs, though..."

I didn't have a drinking problem except when I couldn't get a drink.

"…but you know what your problem is, Ron? Aside from the mustache, I mean. You think there's such a thing as true love."

"Love is real, you cynical hack," said Ron. "And my mustache is glorious."

"Sure, yeah." Shifty Eyes downed a pint of beer. "But what do people really mean when they talk about it? True love, that is. They mean guaranteed love. You thought Howie was the end of the line for you. Thought you didn't need to worry about things anymore. Things like

Chapter 3—Some Light Errands and Then a Trip to the Movies

When I woke the next morning, I realized that I hadn't told anyone about the fish on my door.

Had it all been a prank? A dream?

Stepping outside, I confirmed that the fish was still there. In fact, it looked healthier than ever. No flies. No putrefaction. A faint, salty aroma. I could have sworn I saw its fins wiggle.

I ran upstairs to the duplex balcony. No dividing wall separated our apartments, only a flimsy railing and a short gap. I hopped the railing and shouted at Ron through his sliding glass door. There was a thump on his bedroom wall adjacent to the balcony, but no answer.

"Hey!" I called again. "Do you remember the Alligator Man from last night? You had to have seen him. Worms in his hands? Shrouded in a dark mist that ate my mind? I think he wants me dead."

Silence.

"Ron, this is important. Someone has damaged my door and left me a threatening…uh, omen. It's a fish."

"Leonard," said Ron, barely loud enough to hear. "Stop talking. I'll be out in a minute."

After ten minutes, Ron shuffled onto the balcony shirtless, a fresh smoke dangling from the side of his mouth.

"How are you not hung over?" he asked.

"Oh, it's coming," I said. "I can feel it."

"And what's this about a fish?"

"Yesterday, I came home from work, and there was a fish on the door. Someone stabbed it there with a knife. A fucking knife, Ron."

"Why didn't you tell me this yesterday?"

"Because I wanted to have fun! But the fish is still there. Have you ever heard of something like this?"

Ron puked over the balcony. "Gimme a minute."

One minute turned into a power nap. We both suffered backlogs of acetaldehyde in our bodies.

When we eventually made it to my door, Ron and I stood contemplating the fish for a long while.

"I don't think that fish is dead," said Ron.

"I don't think so either," I agreed.

"That might be a magical fish. I mean, that's for-sure a magical knife, so this is probably a magical fish."

"What makes you think the knife is magical?"

"Experience." Ron inspected the weapon gingerly, even smelled it. "The design is rudimentary, with no power source, no modules, and no circuits. The blade is made from silver. Only mancers deal with that kind of nonsense."

"Fishmancers."

"Yup, probably Fishmancers."

"You don't suppose we're being a little…reductive?" I asked.

"What? Magic fish. Magic knife. There's no such thing as a knifemancer, and Fishmancers are, you know, famous for their aquatic animals."

"Yeah, but that doesn't mean they *did* this. Anybody can buy a magic knife or a magic fish."

Ron sucked his teeth. "You're talking out your ass on that one. Fishmancers and Birdmancers and Fungusmancers are all very protective of their familiars. They don't sell them to normies like us."

"All the more reason why they wouldn't stab one to my door!"

"Good point. It seems we have a mystery on our hands."

"It's clearly a threat, right?"

"No doubt about that."

"Where are you going?"

"Inside." He waved goodbye. "I have to puke again, and then I need to sleep for another sixteen hours."

"But I might be in danger," I called.

"Don't worry, I'll protect you," he replied, halfway into his apartment.

"But you're hungover. And asleep."

"If someone comes to the house, just wake me up and I'll kill them."

"What if there's no time?"

"Don't you have a gun?"

"I'm an Expert Support Miscellaneous. It's not in my spec."

Ron disappeared inside but kept the door open with his foot. "Now might be a good time to invest in a primary weapon."

"But I don't have any money!" I shouted as his door slammed shut.

That's when I noticed the briefcase that had been shoved into my empty terracotta planter, which I hauled down from the Garden of Terror many years ago. One of my first jobs, in fact. Why hadn't I planted anything in it yet?

I just about shit myself when I opened the briefcase.

It was filled with money. And so many *kinds* of money.

Bills, coins, exotic meal vouchers, ingots, bearer bonds, stock certificates, cowrie shells, mail-in-rebates, and more jewels than you could shake a stick at. This was no ordinary briefcase-filled-with-money. This was an Interdimensional Freelancer's briefcase.

My entire career, people asked me why I opted for a Designation like Expert Support Miscellaneous. Support was bad enough to a red-blooded adventurer. But Miscellaneous? Might as well settle for Caddy, they said.

The answer to their mocking inquiries lay in this disparate collection of financial instruments unceremoniously jammed in my planter.

Lunatics. Autocrats. Fanatics. Demi-gods and literal monsters. A billion factions vied for supremacy over the Multiverse. They came in many stripes and flavors, but all were depressingly common in their pursuit of wealth. Accumulation without end. But at one time, peoples and planets and dimensions were joined by equitable exchange, rather than corporate or political consolidation. Rare individuals, the vanguards of this brief golden age. Principled—for the most part—and driven by curiosity more than profit. Erudite merchant-adventurers known as Interdimensional Freelancers. The first to chart the Levels without violence.

In time, the best among them were destroyed, the rest swallowed up by wealth and power beyond reason.

I became an adventurer for many reasons, but to be to like the early Interdimensional Freelancers was in my top five. An Expert Support Miscellaneous couldn't compete, but nothing else came as close.

And now this briefcase.

Nobody ever accused me of being the sharpest stick in the punji pit, but even I couldn't deny that a lot of weird shit was being left on my doorstep without explanation. Almost as if someone *wanted* me to freak out and buy a gun.

Which, of course, I very much wanted to do.

My friends didn't remember it well, but I once owned a primary weapon. A big, double-action revolver with a silver finish and a logogram that read "facilitator" engraved on its barrel—or more accurately, "that which facilitates thy will."

No one sold the right cartridges, of course. All I ever had were the six that came with the gun. My reluctance to employ its power ensured its uselessness, save the first and only time it was fired.

On that occasion, I leveled the mighty Facilitator, squeezed the trigger, and was immediately knocked unconscious by the barrel as the gun recoiled in my hands. It proved a lifesaving accident. If I had remained upright, the colossal tegu from Level 43 would have impaled me with its tongue.

After that encounter, I sold the revolver to pay the mortgage, which seemed a better investment at the time

There was nothing for it. I would have to go straight to the Fishmancers and demand an explanation. And to do that, I would need to be armed.

It was time to visit Araxi's Pawn & Gun.

"I don't know what you are," I told the fish on my door, which continued to goggle at me. "but we're in this together now."

I stowed the fish in a canvas bag, careful not to remove the dagger from the body in case it was a trap, which was usually the case with magical things.

Central Plaza was happening. Adventuring parties everywhere—people returning from the Levels covered in filth, their expressions like extinguished matches, some of them hauling loot, some of them not. Those waiting to ascend were mad with bloodlust, treasure-lust, and other foul impulses, heedless of danger.

"I know what I'm doing," we always said.

The door to Araxi's Pawn & Gun was made of iron. I opened it as if breaching a barricade. A dark interior perfumed with frankincense greeted me, the walls lined with every weapon imaginable: crossbows, miniguns, jeweled scimitars, handwritten poetry, mustard gas, even black boxes with notes that said things like "Don't open until Saturnalia" and "I've always loved you."

As usual, an old dog woman named Rolla stood guard behind a display case full of power gauntlets at the front of the store. Dogfolk were usually such athletic creatures—like whips with teeth—but Rolla was all pug, her silver muzzle sunk deep in ornery wrinkles, a hoop of fat around her neck.

"Good morning," I said to her. "Is Araxi in?"

"Take a look around, Dingleberry Jones," she replied, glancing at me with disdain.

"Will do," I said. "Always a pleasure."

"Get bent."

Things were busy but I didn't have to wait long. Araxi spied me hovering and beckoned me over. She was mean and sweet, like a marshmallow stuffed with fishbones. She had long black hair and a third eyeball squinting on her forehead. She always dressed in dark leather clothes that were endlessly popular on Mezzanine. I often wondered if she was an ex-Muni.

"What a surprise," said Araxi. "I haven't seen you here since you pawned that beautiful gun. I thought you'd given up adventuring."

"I was just taking a break from armed combat."

She snorted. "You're as bad at lying as you are at fighting."

I dropped my briefcase on the counter. "The ultimate weapon is cash."

Araxi whistled when I opened the lid. "Dare I ask how or where you acquired all of this?"

"I have my ways."

All three of her eyes narrowed with disappointment. "Doing wetwork for the Syndicate now? Or is the Anti-Guild back in town?"

"I'm not a fucking moron, Araxi."

"So you say. But I know the kind of jobs you've been getting. If it's not dirty, then what is it?"

I thought about lying. "I found this in my planter."

"Oh, Leonard."

"It's not booby-trapped. And there's no tracking device on it."

"There ought to be." Araxi plucked a banded black stone from one of the compartments. "This is emperor onyx. Currency on Level 99."

"I didn't know the Liches used currency," I said, amazed. "Who would they even trade with?"

"Who indeed?" she said, dropping the stone back in the case. "This belonged to someone either very dangerous or very foolish."

"I'll go with foolish since they lost an entire briefcase full of cheddar."

She leaned an elbow on the counter and regarded me dryly. "Leonard, honey, you should consider the possibility that something about this whole situation is amiss." "Fishy, you might even say."

"…I might."

I checked the room for guys in identical black armor. "Yesterday, someone put a fish on my door."

Her expression darkened.

"It was knifed right into the door. I feel like I'm supposed to know what it means, but I've never heard of such a thing. I have it if you wanna see it."

She looked alarmed. "You brought that thing with you?"

"What was I supposed to do, leave it up there?" I held open the canvas bag for her. "I don't recognize the species. Don't know why they used such a nice dagger either. They could have pinned it with a spike. Or maybe just put it in a brown bag and lit it on fire."

She affixed me with her stare. "That's a Mana Fish. And it's been impaled with a silver blade to keep it in stasis so it won't teleport to safety."

"I knew it had to be magic."

"More to the point, Mana Fish are tightly regulated by the Guild, not to mention what the Fishmancers would do if they heard you were schlepping one around in a grocery bag."

"So, you *don't* think the Fishmancers did this?"

"Uh, no. I think someone is in deep shit with the Circle of Magi and they're trying to frame you. And what do you wanna bet it also involves an attaché case filled with rare and exotic currencies?"

I shut the briefcase, or attaché case, or whatever it was called. "I'm not giving this to the Guild."

"Leonard, think rationally for a second."

"I am thinking rationally. That fish was probably on my door for twenty-four hours. I might not have much time before its owner finds me. Same with the money. I might as well spend what I can now and arm myself."

"But if you went to the Guild, they could conduct an investigation." Her third eye glowed ever so slightly. "They could protect you."

"Nuts to that," I said with a grin. "I'm supposed to be an adventurer. This is the most interesting thing that's happened to me in months."

She bit her lip. "Let me ask around. I have clout, I can probably dig up an answer. In the meantime, don't do anything too flashy with the money. And keep that damn thing hidden. Bury it in the backyard. Don't take the dagger out either."

"Speaking of weapons, how about a gun?" I extracted a stack of Municipal certificates—which were significantly more stable than funbucks and much-preferred on Mezzanine. "What will this get me?"

Araxi snatched them up. "If you're fixing to have a stern talk with 'mancers, you'll need anti-magic. This here's a bubblegum special."

I was offered a small, bulbous pistol made of crayon-colored bonbons.

"This thing is ridiculous," I said.

"You bet your ass. It's candymancy. The only thing that can counter magic is more magic, and Candymancers are the only Designation willing to oblige. This little mother deploys .25 caliber self-empowering counterspell gum pellets that will nullify any hex, curse, malediction, enchantment, transmutation, jinx, phantasm, hoodoo, thaumaturgy, talisman, or word of chaos that it touches. Keep it away from your favorite gear. It doesn't counter wishes or sins. But then nothing does."

The weapon felt tacky like old gum. "How does the rest of the magical community feel about you selling these?"

"Exceptionally negative," she replied with a smile. "Keep it out of sight until you need it."

—

Dead Tomas and I went to the movies. We were going to see *Grave Digging in Dreamland*, an early and little-known work from the same director who made *Quimby Goes to Sex Town*, which I hadn't seen either.

"Side by side, you can see that both films explore similar themes," explained Dead Tomas. "Memory, multiplicity, hyper-reality, the intersections between, etcetera. And you can see how the director's style has evolved from one film to the next. But I think *Grave Digging* is a much rawer work of art, filled with honesty and bursts of emotion that you just don't get with *Quimby*. Is it as entertaining? Maybe not. But guys like us, we understand there's more to film than raw entertainment."

I didn't know that at all. As far as I understood, movies were supposed to tantalize by depicting as much sex and violence as they could cram into ninety minutes. In fact, I'd never seen a movie without a number or a body part in the title. I thought it best to withhold judgement.

The mall was on the outskirts of town, and looked always like it was about to be demolished. Dirty floors. Broken lightbulbs. A pervasive sense of despair. There were several functioning businesses, but most of the retail space was locked away behind steel shutters, never to open again. Walls were lined with advertisements. "Coming soon!" they declared over bright banners of people eating, gambling, wrestling in jelly pits. None of the promised attractions ever arrived. The mall was a corpse of commerce, which explained Tomas' attraction to it.

But they did have soft pretzels.

We eventually came upon the movie theater, tucked in behind the food court and the remnants of an indoor amusement park intended for children. In all the years I'd lived in Castaway, I never saw anyone younger than late adolescence. I myself had arrived a young man, I think. The absence of kids never bothered me. In fact, I would have been outraged if I saw them in town. The Levels were dangerous after all. But now, seeing the derelict carousel and broken-down machines with their forgotten cartoon faces, it stirred something ugly inside.

Dead Tomas snapped me out of my thoughts.

"Can you believe this crap?" he demanded.

The crumbling movie theater marquee was in the process of being altered by a tiny robot. It swapped out *Revegenerance 5* for something called *Dick Darkness 3: Swingin' Dicks.*

"Everything has to be a fucking franchise now," said Dead Tomas, lips peeled back in disgust. "*Dick Darkness 2: Electric Boogaloo* was a perfectly adequate follow-up to a fun, if predictable, noir musical about an android stripper programmed to be a detective. The sequel answered all of our questions about the Illuminati and entirely resolved the conflict with Dick's evil sensei slash adoptive father, Dr. Dangerous. There were no loose threads! There were so many other movies that could have used a part three, but not this one."

I vaguely recalled watching the original *Dick Darkness* but wasn't aware they'd made any sequels. The realization that this fictional universe had moved on without me sent a wave of anxiety through my innards.

We were assailed by the stench of burnt popcorn, vegetable oil, and cigarettes as we entered the lobby. The carpet was worn to shreds. The coming attractions posters were centuries-old. The staff consisted of just two punks dressed in red suits and pillbox hats. If they saw us enter, they didn't care. They were too busy arguing.

"I'm telling you he won't make it," said Punk One. "We've seen this a million times."

"How you exaggerate," his coworker replied.

"Thousands of times. Tens of thousands of times."

"This one is different," insisted Punk Two. "I can feel it."

"You always say the same thing," Punk One moaned with the exasperation of a spouse. "You stare at the ocean, gasping with each wave that crests, 'Ooo, this one for sure—this one's different!' None of them are different. We've watched a million waves break on the shore and it'll be a million plus one very soon."

"And you, my friend, stare only at the shallows," said Punk Two with unflappable tenderness. "You watch the tide roll in and out, oblivious to the monstrous body of water beyond. So many waves have ended the same way that you no longer question their passing. You've dulled your imagination. Death cannot tell you about life."

"Death is the entire point of life," Punk One declared. "Or used to be. The tide is certain."

"Until that day when the tide pulls back too far," said Punk Two. "And a great wave drowns you beneath its uncaring fury."

"I'll eat my hat if that ever happens. But soft, the customers approach."

Dead Tomas leaned on the candy counter with both elbows, dropping globules of flesh all over the scratched-up glass. "Sorry to interrupt your philosophizing, boys, but we'd like to buy some tickets."

Punk One, snaggletooth and endowed with a frizzy mane of hair, sneered at Tomas. "Why of course, your majesty. That happens to be the exact reason we're here: to sell tickets. And what a thrill it is to see our efforts bear fruit."

"I apologize for my coworker," said Punk Two, who was shorter and more conventionally handsome. "We're just so bored."

"Do you know how many people go out to the movies in this town?" asked Punk One. "Zip. Zero. Bagel. Castaway is *full* of assholes. Not you guys, though. You're cool. You're so cool I won't even charge admission. Would you like some popcorn? Maybe a beverage? We have whiskey."

I burped. "I'll take a Springle."

"We don't have any fucking Springle. We have booze. And cola."

"We also have slushies," offered Punk Two.

"Absolutely not," I said. "How about a malt beer?"

Punk One slapped a can of Dizzy Dame on the counter. "No charge for the cool guy."

"Uh, thanks," I said, unsure of this new sobriquet.

"No," said Punk One, leveling a finger-gun at me, "thank you, Leon Marcs."

"His name is Leonard," said Dead Tomas.

"Sure, whatever," said Punk One, not looking at him. "Thanks so much."

"What are you thanking me for?" I demanded.

"For all that you've done," said Punk One. "For all that you might do."

"For all that you *will* do," Punk Two emphasized. "We believe in you, Leopold Marcs. We think you'll make the right decision."

"Speak for yourself," said Punk One. "I think Leo's gonna die."

"It's Leonard," I corrected.

Dead Tomas looked sideways at me. "You come here often?"

"I've never met these punks in my life," I said.

"He doesn't have a clue," said Punk One to his coworker. "He's just another copy. An ersatz Lenny Marcs. The real guy is lost forever."

"Or maybe the real Levon Marcs never was," said Punk Two. "Maybe life is just an endless series of facsimiles. The one that becomes many. True originality dwells only within the collective multitudes, then. Bulletproof. Unkillable. Recycled until the cycle continues no more."

I tapped the glass for emphasis. "My. Name. Is. Leonard."

"See that annoyed look on his face?" Punk One asked his coworker. "That's probably how his wife feels. Every time."

"Every ding-dong time," Punk Two agreed.

Punk One opened the till and slammed it shut again. "Two tickets coming right up. One for you, the great Leonardo Marcs, and one for you, hideous embodiment of our arrogance towards nature. Enjoy the show, you guys."

I stared at the flimsy paper ticket. "How did you know what movie we wanted to see?"

"There's only one movie worth seeing," said Punk Two breezily.

Dead Tomas drummed his fingers. "I'd like a malt beer."

"That was our last one," said the Punks in unison.

"A slushie, then," said Tomas sadly.

"No!" I could feel the sound of it—the slurping—in my bones. "Just have this Dizzy Dame. I don't want it. I don't want anything."

"Are you sure?" Punk Two looked concerned. "Nothing?"

"I didn't say there was nothing I wanted. I want what you don't have."

"Ah!" Punk Two winked at Punk One. "So not for nothing, not for everything, but for the one thing."

"The one right thing," said Punk One sagely.

I rubbed the bridge of nose. "I'm tired of people acting like they know me. Like they're working on something big. What have you got going on? You work at a movie theater."

"I hear what you're saying." Punk Two winked at me now, which I didn't care for at all. "Always be patient."

"Everything is not spoken in code," I said.

"Sure it is," said Punk One. "You think the sounds you're making—with your teeth and face meat and lungs and whatnot—would be worth a damn if we didn't have the cipher in our brains? We're all transmitting secrets. You, my friend, are in the shit now."

"I'm not your friend. I'm not in the shit." I took Dead Tomas by the arm. "Let's get to this fucking movie."

"The end is not the beginning!" Punk Two yelled at our backs. "You make your future. Not the tide. Not the Company. Not anyone but you."

"Wrong, it's all bullshit," called Punk One. "The future is written in the past and the past is dead. An ouroboros of death. Inevitable. Eternal. Immutable."

I gave them both the finger.

Tiny, bioluminescent mushrooms led us to our seats and clicked off when we sat. The darkness of the theater was so heavy. It condensed on my skin and soaked into my clothes.

The crack of the Dizzy Dame reverberated in my ears.

Dead Tomas smacked his lips. "I chugged benzene last night and it tasted better than this."

I couldn't see my hands. "Those guys back there. What were they talking about? How come they knew me?"

"Don't let those knuckleheads get to you, Leonard."

"First the Alligator Man. And now those punks…"

Dead Tomas rubbed my shoulder. "Relax, pal. It's movie time."

My eyeballs were useless knobs on my face as I strained to see him in the dark. "Does the name 'El Savel' mean anything to you?"

He didn't answer.

"I might be losing my mind, Tomas."

"Shush, it's starting!"

The first flashes on the screen were high voltage static that singed our nerves and scrambled our brains, stealing everything but our fear.

Establishing shots were employed. Angles manipulated. Shifts in tone were signaled by color instead of musical stings. How was I supposed to know what to feel if the soundtrack didn't tell me?

The plot, such as it was, revolved around a smuggler trying to pull off one last job so he could win back his estranged wife. Sound and lighting continuity were not preserved. Characters were introduced and then forgotten. Shots of a sunset were crudely interspersed while a baby carriage went hurtling down a great set of stairs, never to be addressed. Most of the extras were played by cardboard cutouts. A risky casting choice.

It was all very symbolic, but when the main character turned to the camera and said, "Leonard, it's me, Leonard. I'm in this movie but you won't recognize me. The Ninth Lathe of Heaven waits where you dare to tread—find it before it's too late. I sent you something that should help," I knew that I was never going to be a movie buff. Some things were just too artsy for me.

In the end, the protagonist abandoned his life of crime to spend more time with his kids, but not before shattering a mirror and beating his own reflection to death in a brutal, expletive-filled showdown that lasted fifteen and a half minutes. The corpse was buried inside a dream that might have been his dream all along.

Credits rolled and the lights clicked on. We were the only ones in the auditorium. The place had felt so grand in the dark, but now everything looked dingy and small under the house lights.

"So, Leonard, did you find it?" asked Tomas.

I glared at him. "What's your angle, you motherfucker? Did those punks put you up to this?"

He had his lip out. "I asked 'how did you find the movie.' Entertaining?"

"Oh," I said, embarrassed. "Yes, I liked it. It was different. The movies I watch usually make a lot more sense. But it can be good to embrace nonsensical things. Life is like that."

"Just because you don't recognize the tropes in a film doesn't mean it was nonsensical," chided Dead Tomas. "That's like saying a language is nonsensical because you can't speak it."

"Don't tell me what is or isn't the right interpretation. I'll fuck you up. Do you hear me? You have no idea who you're messing with."

Part of his ear rotted off. "You're in a bad mood."

The theater's ceiling was liver-spotted with water damage and I blew a raspberry at it. "Let's get drunk again."

"What about work?"

"What about it?" I said. "I don't have a job."

"We're going to Level 2," he said, as if it were the most reasonable thing in the world. "You and me, tomorrow. We're getting donuts first. Did you forget?"

"Tomas, I forget everything. It's what I do."

"I'm excited to kill goblins with you," he said.

"You don't kill them." I leaned back in the seat, closed my eyes, and considered taking a nap right there. "You just…beat them up. They're kind of like your coworkers."

Dead Tomas reclined next to me. "I'm excited to be your coworker."

Chapter 4—Before Leonard Came to Castaway

I had a life before I came to Castaway. Before I forgot everything.

This was me.

—

I had left the dilapidation of student housing and moved back in with my mom, for I had no money. And being single, friendless, unemployed, and obsessed with a mummified piece of my father's forearm, upon which a crude tattoo of an eel had been inked—salvaged against my mother's will, of course—I was in hell.

A standard vocational degree from Salvar Polytechnic wasn't much, but if I was clever, it could be enough to get me started in Bastion City. The Big Apple. The Center of the Multiverse.

My babyface reflection scowled at me from the bathroom mirror.

"Hello, mother," I said to my reflection. "I'm off to the big city, and that's all there is to it. Don't try to stop me."

My reflection was unconvinced.

"Mother, I'm going away. Not for long. Just a few decades. Possibly until the day I die. Love you! Call soon."

My reflection pursed its lips in defiance.

"Now see here, mumsy: I'm leaving this one-horse town behind and there's not a damn thing you can do about it. Whaddya think about that? Just try and stop me. I'll rip off your head."

My reflection shook its head. You can't talk to your mother like that.

"If I betray weakness, she'll guilt me into staying."

My reflection shrugged.

I was doing the right thing. I knew it. But I was gonna break her heart all the same. I had to be caring, yet resolute.

I glared at myself. "You can do this."

As usual, Amanda Marcs was hunched over her keyboard, her face inches from the monitor. She traded in a broad spectrum of financial instruments, commanding a portfolio as diverse as it was treacherous. Fortunes were made, spent, resurrected, and warehoused, her positions leveraged over thousands of derivatives. A mistake could undo years of progress. Her employers were invested in a game that spanned generations.

I approached slowly and loudly but she didn't seem to notice.

"Mom." I cleared my throat. "Mom. Look at me."

"What is it, Lenny?" She declined to look up.

"We need to talk about something."

"It can wait." Her nose got even closer to the screen. "Good news at least? Something to make me smile?"

I hesitated.

"Then don't bother."

I stood close and touched her boney shoulder. "I'm not attending the academy. I've decided to do something else. I'm going to Bastion City."

She rolled her shoulder away from my hand. "Is that so? And what will you do when you get there? How will you make a living?"

"Trading. Like you. But in hard commodities."

"With what capital?"

"I was thinking something hands-on. A field consultant."

Her fingers froze. "Field consultant?"

I'd said too much.

At last, she turned and looked at me with her dark little eyes. "You mean adventuring. You want to be an adventurer."

I nodded at my reflection in her glasses.

"This has something to do with that *thing*, doesn't it?" she said. "That wretched keepsake of yours."

"It's a talisman, mom."

"Most people carry photos of the departed, not the desiccated remains of their ugly tattoos."

"I guess that makes me different," I said.

"It makes you a fucking crazy person. Not that I should be surprised."

"Don't start that again."

"Does it whisper to you at night, Leonard? Do you hear your

father's voice emanating from it? I begged him not to get it, you know. I told him he was dabbling in the occult, that he was putting his soul at risk. He ignored me of course. He got that snake right on his arm. Right where I would have to look at it."

"Heavenly Bogo is an eel," I said.

"Do not speak its ridiculous name to me! I used to think chlamydia was the worst thing Lionel could bring home, but if I'd known insanity was contagious, I would've killed him myself."

"Dad's been dead for years. When are you going to stop blaming him for everything?"

Mother rose from her chair, far shorter than me, yet she filled the room with her presence. "Never. And if I see him in the Afterlife, I'll make him dead again. Your father didn't care about us. While I worked like a dog, he was out porking his way through the Levels. Every princess and bar wench what looked at him sideways. Hardly earned a dime. You have no idea what I put myself through to give us a decent life."

"I'm not trying to defend him," I said, honest. "But he's dead. I wish you would recognize that and move on."

"Is that what this is all about?" Mother pointed her chin at the locket containing dad's tattoo. "Is this how you're going to move on, Leonard? You carry Lionel's skin around and play adventurer, and you think maybe that will heal you?"

I had to pretend she wasn't correct. "The eel is the key to something important. Something much greater than us."

"And to what treasure could such a thing possibly be the key?"

"It's not just a tattoo. This is a depiction of the Ninth Lathe of Heaven."

"Holy fuck," she said.

"I know you don't believe—"

"What in the balls am I supposed to believe?" she shouted. "That an evil corporation wants to rule the Multiverse using the living relics of some dead god? Big deal. Belief's got nothing to do with it. Monsters and tyrants are everywhere. Even if it were true—which it isn't—it wouldn't change a goddamn thing. You can't fight evil like that. None of us can. It's vanity to pretend otherwise."

I soaked in her ire. "It's not important that you believe me. Because it won't change my mind. I'm going to Bastion City, and that's all there is to it."

She sighed. "I was sure I'd never hear another word of Lionel's bullshit when he died, because the one thing he promised was that he wouldn't drag you into it. I guess he lied about that too."

"You were the one who gave me his journals."

"I didn't give them to you. I allowed you to keep them, the way I let you keep that gruesome little memento. I thought—stupidly—that you might see your father for what he was. I thought you were smarter than him."

"Mom, please."

"Don't touch me. No, get away, Leonard! Do you hate me so much? Do you hate this home? Then go. Go to Bastion City. The sooner the better."

This was my opportunity to make a clean break. The moment that could have sent me on my way.

I should have just turned around and left.

"I'm not leaving because I hate you," I said, trying to get her to look at me. "You've let your bitterness swallow you up, and I can't live with it anymore."

She stared at the corner.

"You loved dad knowing what he was, and you believed in him once. You could have thrown his stuff away—destroyed the tattoo—but you didn't."

Her eyes sank to the floor.

I tried to catch her gaze. "I just want to be free."

We stood in silence.

"Go then," she said at last. "And be free."

I couldn't move.

"What? Were you expecting more? Did you want me to break down in tears? I have my dignity, Leonard. Go and be done with me."

I couldn't look away.

"Why do you stare at me, child? What more could you want?"

"I'm not doing this to hurt you," I whispered. "I love you."

"You don't know anything about love. But you will. And I hope you remember me when it happens. I hope you remember every terrible detail. Because if you don't, things will end for you the way they did for Lionel and me. If I have any goodwill left, it's that I hope I never see you again."

Mom sat down at her monitor and resumed typing. It was a long time before I left. She didn't turn around, even when I said my last goodbye.

—

The velocitized landscape moved in slow motion as the maglev soared over the desert at a frictionless five hundred miles an hour. Overnight, a rare rainstorm had sent the wildflowers into bloom. A verdant field that stretched all the way to the Bastion Plateau. The flowers would soon wither, sapped of their precious moisture by the sun, but for now, anything seemed possible.

Even on a planet as advanced as Unity, ancient mass transit remained the most reliable method of conveyance. Paradigmatic subversion—the basis for any transdimensional portal—was too expensive for most applications. Not that I minded. An incredible excitement germinated within me and I felt lighter with each hour that passed on the train. I didn't want it to stop.

Someone stumbled into my booth and nearly sat in my lap. He was thin and disheveled, dressed in an oversized coat and a hat with roses in the brim.

"Sorry about that," he said when he'd regained his composure. "Low blood sugar. Can't always keep my balance."

"That's alright," I said. "Would you like a seat?"

"No, thank you." He popped some candy in his mouth. "I noticed you have a couple bags here, and a far-off look in your eyes. May I ask: are you migrating to the City?"

I thought about lying. "Yeah."

The man's face erupted in a smile. "This is your lucky day. My name's El Savel and I have been tasked by the Order of the Sublime Reliquary to welcome migrants such as yourself to our wonderful town. May I ask: do you have accommodations lined up?"

Who was I to interrupt a good sales pitch? I shook my head.

"Not uncommon," said El Savel. "The Order of the Sublime Reliquary recognizes the diverse needs of all migrants, refugees, asylees, and visitors. We operate a state-of-the art capsule hotel off Sanguine Street. You provide us a small amount of information—the reasons for your travel, work history, biometric data, etcetera—and we grant you a five-night stay at our wonderful facility."

"What's the catch?"

El Savel chuckled warmly. "Bastion City is a popular destination. Looking for work takes time. After your complimentary stay is over, you'll find that our prices are very reasonable. I guarantee you'll find a similar offer nowhere else."

"That data you collect, how much do you get for selling it?"

His smile didn't falter. "More than you'd think. The Order of the Sublime Reliquary believes that investing in new arrivals is the best way to develop the community and grow our network of allies."

"I assume you get kickbacks from the temp agencies as well."

"Only if the temp keeps the gig," he said. "They won't pay for junkies or morons. Too many people mistake the sophistication of our social programs for largesse. They are rudely disabused of these foolish views."

"And how long does the average migrant stay in one of your coffins before going crazy?"

"Some disappear after a few months. Some move on to better things. And some just get used to capsule life. They sell their meatspace to the Pan-Dimensional Network and live online fulltime. For a nominal fee, we keep them on liquids and roll them around so they don't get bedsores."

"That's fucked up," I said.

"That's the least of it in our wonderful, fucked-up town." El Savel thrust a clipboard at me. "Don't act like you're going to turn this offer down. Believe me, it's better than the shelters. Good food, but they *will* process you, and there's no telling where you'll end up when that happens."

I took the clipboard. "Show me your favorite bar."

"Oh, you drink, huh?" He watched me write my name. "Come to The Lounge sometime. Coordinates 48°N 125°W—about two blocks relative-southeast from the laundromat. I'm there most nights."

"You got any friends? Can you introduce me to a girl?"

"You're a fast one. Start with The Lounge. Maybe meet some nice folks. We'll have a ball."

He took a blood sample and examined my info.

Satisfied, he handed me five paper tickets.

"Welcome to Bastion City, Leonard Marcs. You just bought yourself a hundred and twenty hours of freedom. Make them count."

With a tip of his hat, El Savel wandered off to find his next commission.

The maglev rounded a red stone butte and passed through a portal without warning. The desert and its wide-open sky were obliterated by a single structure, a dark cuboid fifty miles tall, floating in a bottomless sea of variegated clouds. Engraved into its edifice were Tetragrammic symbols that glittered like stained glass. Its composite superstructure had withstood everything from dragon attacks to hydrogen bombs. Not even the Old Ones could touch this place.

We had arrived at Bastion City.

The maglev deposited us at a spiked protrusion called the Port Authority. Deboarding the train, I stepped almost instantaneously into line. The place was packed with a full sampling of the Multiverse. Intelligent races I had only read about in fiction. I wanted to look calm and collected, but I had never seen so many varieties of sapient life before.

Goatfolk, dogfolk, frogfolk, bovines, centaurs, sciapods, moon sharks, puppets, scarecrows, goblins, funguspeople, sentient crystals, sentient gasses, cloud-conscious utility fog, trans-species cyborgs, a myriad array of insectoids, undead, blackbirds, octopi, crabs in power armor, rockfolk, and many, many others.

"Passports!" hollered an elephantine creature in a trench coat. "Get your passports here! Won't get into Bastion City without a valid photo ID. Quick turnarounds. Ready in as little as fifteen minutes!"

The line moved at a glacial pace, granting me ample opportunity to be accosted by hawkers and crapmongers.

"Mobile currency exchange coming through, folks. Your money's no good here. Gotta get them authentic Bastion City dollars. Favorable rates available. Get your free credit report now."

The koalaperson in front of me gazed at a pair of gold coins in her hand and waved the currency vendor over.

"Very fine Union drachmas, ma'am." The vendor fondled the coins, weighing them against six copper rods in his other hand. "After commission, your total is eight hundred and twenty dollars."

The koala looked stricken. "*Pha'o lat. Zeŋ'amma tu ade Sorbu-Chás.*"

The vendor wrinkled his nose. "No speak-a the Universal, huh?"

I cleared my throat at him. "She says she's from the Serene Union Commonwealth."

"You speak gibber-gabber?" asked the vendor, relieved. "Tell her she can have eight hundred for the drachmas."

"You said eight hundred and twenty before." I reminded him.

"I'll give you ten for your trouble." The vendor winked.

"*Ke toas'e chenko badessti,*" I told the woman. "*No'amma—*"

"*Sorbu plasi,*" the koala interjected. "*Ne'o dewoti ahn kre-chenko baw'quandi. Bebba tu quandi.*"

"She knows you've made a mistake," I said. "These are ducats from the Serene Union Commonwealth, not drachmas from the Stellar Union. They bear a strong resemblance, but here on the obverse is the dogaressa herself."

"How careless of me," said the vendor, glaring. "In that case, ma'am, we're looking at twelve hundred dollars. Can you translate that?"

The koala and I broke out into simultaneous exhortations.

"One at a time!" roared the vendor. "I don't speak gobbledygook."

"It's not Gobbledygook," I said. "It's Interface. More common than most Universal dialects."

"Thanks for the lesson," said the vendor, not meeting my gaze. "Tell her I'm offering twelve hundred."

"That can't be right," I told him. "Each of these ducats contains thirteen grams of ultra-pure gold. The spot price alone—"

"This isn't a bullion shop, kid." The vendor looked as if he might walk away, but his greed won out. "The Bastion City dollar is pegged to a broad-basket of interdimensional currencies, not the price of gold. I'm prepared to give this anthro-marsupial one thousand two hundred and eleven Bastion City dollars and forty cents for a pair of cumbersome antiques. She can take it or leave it."

The koala stepped away from the merchant.

I smirked at him. "Looks like she wants a counteroffer. I'm sure there are plenty of exchanges on the other side. Someone with a business license maybe."

In a frozen slice of time, somewhere between the pressure of his fist and the pain of impact, I acknowledged the raw fact that I was being punched in the face. My brain hoped that this realization would help soften the blow.

It did not.

Blood pounded in my ears as I scrambled away, trying to put distance between my face and his fists. A crowd formed around us, their boredom morphing swiftly into bloodlust. The koala shouted encouragement at me in a pidgin of Universal and her native Interface.

The vendor pulled a knife. "You little scumbag. I'm a fucking taxpayer. Who the hell are you? Another transient come to live on the dole?"

I couldn't stop myself from speaking. "I hope you suffer an emotional rift with your spouse that culminates in a painful divorce, leaving you destitute and bitter for the rest of your life."

The vendor lunged.

My short, stupid little life flashed before my eyes.

The next thing I knew, the merchant was at my feet, his limbs twitching uselessly, a taser prong stuck in his back.

I kicked his dagger away.

Two security bots approached, one of them controlling the taser, the other ready with a net. They walked on four segmented limbs that ended in points, their heads as smooth and round as eggs, faceless and uncaring. The crowd melted away without protest as the unconscious currency vendor was dragged off.

The koala regarded me with shining eyes. We exchanged a few words, but said little after that. Security briefly interrogated us about the incident, but had everything on camera. No charges were to be filed on my part. This was not the vendor's first infraction.

Things got quiet and boring again, though at least I had a pounding headache to entertain me. We saw an uptick in four-legged robot patrols, scanning everyone they passed, occasionally pausing to analyze someone. I passed the time cataloguing all the things that Bastion City might want to quarantine.

Parasites. Bacteria. Explosives. Self-replicating narcotics. Viruses. Mold spores. Ad-tech. Prions. Rogue nanites. Garmonbozia. Unethical fruits.

I didn't want to think about how I could have died waiting in customs.

As we shuffled deeper into the depths of the Port Authority, the size and lethality of the security bots increased. They watched us like gargoyles from scaffolding. By the time the turnstiles were in sight, the robots had grown ten sizes, more resembling the violent mecha of ancient times.

The koala approached the customs desk and got through without incident. She waved goodbye to me.

The customs officer, an authoritarian strain of human being, looked at my passport like he'd never seen one before. "Son, what is your polity or corporate holdingship of origin?"

"The Municipal Alliance," I said

"Never heard of it."

I balked. "You haven't? It was a founding member—"

"Please describe the purpose of your trip," continued the customs officer.

"I'm an immigrant. That's my visa right there."

"I know what a visa looks like, son. Tell me, does everyone in the so-called Municipal Alliance speak Universal, or just you?"

"It's a multinational, interstellar, interdimensional federation of city states."

The customs officer leaned on his elbows, looking hard at me. "You didn't answer the question."

"All of us receive compulsory education in multiple languages."

"*Which* ones? You won't be the first person to claim Universal *and* Universal Basic on their language forms."

"Multiple dialects of Universal are required," I said, trying not to glare, "along with Interface. I also speak Query, Pan-Shogg, and High

Galactic. How many languages do you speak?"

The officer was unmoved. "And you can read in all those?"

"Yes. I can also read five logogrammic schemas."

"Schemas, huh? You're educated, then."

"At the Salvar Polytechnic Vocational School."

"And if I contact that school, they'll verify your degree?"

"Vocational certificate in communications. That's my certificate right there."

The customs officer glanced at it. "How long do you intend to stay in Bastion City?"

"Indefinitely? I'm immigrating."

The customs officer handed my documents back without further perusal. "Insert your finger into the port below."

They drew my blood and scanned my head.

"Low grade hippocampal abnormalities present, but nothing that takes you past threshold. Fully vaccinated. No presence of the LQ1 Virus, but you'll catch it soon enough. A simple analgesic should address most of your symptoms. There's a greater than 0% chance you'll develop tertiary gummas. Please report to a clinic immediately if that happens."

"What the hell's a gumma?"

They went through my luggage with humorless efficiency.

"Mr. Marcs, are you now or have you ever been a member of, or provided material support to, any terrorist organization defined by the United Spacefaring Nations or their observing security members?"

"No. Has anyone ever said yes to that question?"

"Are you now or have you ever been a member of, or provided material support to, any of the following controversial syndicates identified by the United Spacefaring Nations and their observing security members: ExoVerde, Nova Imperator, Incelocalypse, Sons of S.O.N., the Lost City of Atlantis Resort and Spa, the Cray-Rock Cash Call, or the Everybody Company?"

"Is that a complete list of controversial syndicates?"

"Just answer the question."

"No. I've never heard of those groups."

"Mr. Marcs, do you swear to renounce all allegiance and fidelity to any foreign monarch, potentate, corporation, state, or sovereign whatsoever and to henceforth uphold the constitution of the Unitary Republic of Bastion City, in sickness and in health, till death do you part?"

"I do. Yes. With all my heart."

"Then, I now pronounce you a lawful permanent resident. Please kiss the dotted line. Welcome to Bastion City."

Exiting the Port Authority, I saw folks detained behind a laser field and subjected to extra screening measures, their possessions aggressively searched, their bodies prodded and probed. Most of them were human. All of them were clearly part of the Castaway Movement.

"You ask me where my country is, you dog?" roared one of the detainees. "My country is nowhere! It was conquered by the Khanate, annexed by the League, gifted to the Conclave, sold to the Union, and abandoned to pirates and rebels at the first sign of trouble. I have no nation. I am Castaway! There is no database in all the Multiverse that can tell you who I am. Only I have that power."

On the street, I was taken by the splendor of Bastion City.

The first level of the cuboid's interior—the primary habitation level—was a continuous, spherical floor. The city wrapped entirely around itself. At its center was open sky, thousands of towers from above and below jutting into the clouds. Great flocks of birds circled within that rarified space, their multitudinous cries echoing over the din of street traffic. The City had one hell of an air purification system. It was humid like a jungle. I could already feel my taint perspiring.

Cyclopean arcologies loomed out of the low-lying fog and chaotic neighborhoods thrived at their feet. Pedestrians thronged the skywalks or gathered on terraces and arcades. Businesses and attractions occupied every available surface. And where there weren't sapient peoples congregating or passing, there were flowers. Roses. Millions of roses and fruit trees and berry bushes. The smell of growing things was so strong and sweet it was intoxicating. I stumbled along in a fugue of wonder.

I'd be sleeping in a box that night. But seeing and smelling and hearing it all for the first time felt like coming home. The home I was meant to have.

I knew I never wanted to live anywhere else.

—

Five days later, I had submitted hundreds of applications and would need to submit hundreds more while I waited for interviews, if any, to materialize. I couldn't afford to lose momentum. Bastion City would eat me alive.

Just as I finished pulling on pants, there came a scraping sound and my door was thrown wide open. Three orcs, with black security garb stretched across their barreled torsos, pried me out of the coffin. I was afraid to resist them and I couldn't understand a word they were saying.

It soon became obvious they were going to throw me out.

"Hey, is this about the rent? I can pay."

The orcs hoisted me like a trussed pig and carried me down the hall.

"Goddammit, I have money," I said.

The word *money* caught their attention.

"Yes, money. El Savel. See El Savel now."

The orcs bore me to the manager's suite and dumped me on the welcome mat. One of them checked something on his list and they ran off in a dead sprint. Probably to evict someone else.

El Savel shouted at me through the door before I could knock.

He lived onsite, but unlike the rest of us, had his own studio with a kitchenette and private bathroom. When he wasn't soliciting new clients for the Order of the Sublime Reliquary, he could be found smoking a waterpipe filled with delectations. Today, however, I found him seated at his desk—AKA kitchen table—sober and pissed off.

"Leonard," he said, looking much aggrieved behind stacks of dirty dishes, "what part of our arrangement did you fail to understand? I ran your background check myself. I vetted you. That means I put my name on the line. I said to everyone in my network, 'Hey, you can trust this guy, no problem.' We gave you five days. For free. Seventy-two hundred minutes. That's a lot of minutes. More than enough time to get your shit together, wouldn't you agree?"

"There has to be a mistake," I told him. "My ticket just expired."

"No, it expired five minutes ago."

"But that's crazy. I was literally on my way to pay when those goons dragged me out of the capsule."

El Savel sighed and rubbed his temples. "Leonard, I like you. But this is Bastion City. We're not fucking around, baby. You wanna be a tenant here, you gotta pay your rent on time, and I mean that in the strictest sense of the word. You think you can take five minutes away from me? Think again."

I was so taken aback I didn't say a word. I just handed over my debit card, which El Savel charged without comment.

"Hey," he said, suddenly a friend once more, "don't sweat it, big guy. You're all paid up for the next seven days. One hundred and sixty-eight hours. I usually charge a late fee, but since this is your first infraction, I'll let it go." He let me take my card, but held on for a moment longer when I tried to pull away. "And, Leonard, let's not have this conversation again."

My ears burned.

Tears of embarrassment welled in my eyes as I slunk back to my capsule. The orcs had left my door open and someone had already looted my stuff, the remainder of which was left strewn up and down the hallway.

"Today's just not your day," said a woman, poking her head out of her capsule. "You wouldn't believe how desperate some folks are."

I ignored her and collected my things.

"It's a harsh lesson, but you learn quick." Her eyes caught mine. "Pay everything in advance. Never be late. Not even by a minute."

"You don't think this is all a bit extreme?" I said.

"This city looks for excuses to grind people up. Are you crying?"

I shoved the detritus of my belongings back into my capsule as fast as I could. "Nice meeting you, whoever you are."

"Hey, come back, I'm not making fun of you. Crying was like my hobby when I moved here. Things didn't get easier for a long time." She vaulted onto the floor and extended her hand. "I'm Anita."

Her palm was hot. She had big round eyes and an inviting face; her features soft but articulated. Dark hair in a carefree bob. Such an incongruous sight in the dingy and puke-stained flophouse, which stank perpetually of antiseptic and warmed-over food, like maybe it had been a hospital once. Her fragrance cut through it like a knife. Roses.

"I'm about to ask how long you've lived here," I said, "and I'm hoping the answer will be a low number."

"Oh, I like your optimism, sweetcheeks. How long do you think it's been? Do I have that incandescent glow of desperation yet?"

"You look like you're on your way to bigger and better things," I said.

"Almost four years," she replied.

"Holy shit."

"Yeah." She smiled with perverse pride. "Though, to be fair, my work involves a lot of travel. I don't have to hang around here that much."

"Even so. How do you stand it?"

"Most of the neighbors are transients. Migrants minding their own business. Tourists backpacking through the Multiverse. People on their way to bigger and better things, as you might say."

"Or common thieves," I said, glancing into my pilfered capsule.

"Some of that, yeah. The rest aren't even living in meatspace. It's easy to come and go."

"I think I'd rather die than live here that long."

"I used to think so too." She leaned in as though sharing a secret.

"The goal for most people around here is to own an apartment in one of the arcologies. They're all cooperatively controlled by the tenants. Dynastic. Very insular. The only realistic avenue for people like us is to marry into the co-op."

"And were you married long?"

She liked that I caught on. "A few years—time enough to figure out that we had nothing in common. I mean, we were just kids. But the arcologies, people take them so seriously. They're built to last forever, and they can change with their tenants. Self-sufficient, fully automated, everything you could want, wrapped in a neat, utilitarian package. I thought I could maintain my independence. After all, I didn't come here just to spend all my time in one building. But once I stopped going out for little things, it became easier to stay inside for larger things. Soon, going out at all felt tedious and difficult. And that scared me.

"Many of my neighbors hadn't left in years. Some of them had never left at all. Can you imagine? It gave me panic attacks just thinking about it. I've never experienced anything like that level of claustrophobia. Before or since. My ex didn't get it, of course. He thought I was being judgmental. And then he thought I was ungrateful. I used to resent him for it, but I understand why he felt that way now. Our apartment represented our relationship. People in this city move from one building to the next, starting and restarting their lives, but not in the arcologies. That's a permanent move. And people take comfort in that. I didn't. I wasn't ready for it. So, I left, and I rented this coffin. I haven't looked back since.

"My longwinded point," she said, sealing her capsule, "is that it takes time for this city to show you who you are. When it does, you'll know where you belong, but until then, it's best to be in a place like this where the rent is cheap and no one's asking questions. Lose a few things you thought you always needed. And if that doesn't give you some perspective, get out of town while the getting's good."

"Perspective." I chewed on the word. "And have you found it?"

"Why do you think I'm still living in this shithole?" She touched my hand and started for the exit. "See you around, sweetcheeks."

"Have fun at work," I called, knowing not at all if she was going to work or to the mall or to see a friend—or a lover—having literally no idea where she might be headed, but hoping desperately I would see her again.

—

I found a job eventually. A far cry from anything I thought I'd be doing.

My boss, Frick, worked at home in a condominium on the southeastern quantile. He had a mess of kids and a wife nearly half his age who did weddings as a freelance photographer. She also painted.

They seemed happy together.

As the result of an accident that left him with partial face paralysis, Frick had a look of constant surprise. He was, in his own words, a value man. Some years ago, he worked as a cartridge technician at an additive manufacturing superplant but left to start a band. Their group found some moderate success licensing their music, and once the royalties poured in, Frick became obsessed with passive income. From that day forward, he refused to work. He hated that word. Work was for suckers, he'd say. He wanted to own valuable things that did the work for him. He wanted to be a man who owned value.

"Like an investor," I said during my interview.

"No," he replied, deadpan. "Investors are speculators. They try to buy something they think will be valuable later on. I buy things that are valuable now. I'm in the business of value. I cut out the middleman."

Middleman was an important term in Frick's lexicon. Anything detrimental or inconvenient was considered a middleman. Shipping charges were middlemen. Parking tickets were middlemen. His wife was a middleman if she didn't let him get drunk in the afternoons.

"I own websites," explained Frick. "People see the ads. And the longer people stay, the more ads they look at, the more money I make. Simple. I don't have to work for that value. I own that value. I write things on these websites, which creates more value. I write what I know. Articles. Advice columns. Rock n' roll. Relationships. Cheating at golf. Homebrewing. Lycanthropy. I know a little bit about a lot of things. I don't bog myself down with middlemen. I own property. Stocks. Futures. I mine currency. I acquire items people want, then sell them. That's the business model."

"So, like a store?"

"Yeah, I own stores. Five of them. All online."

"And where do you get your stock?"

"People just give things away. People don't understand value the way I do. They let middlemen take advantage of them."

"Must take a lot of work. Finding all that value."

"It's not *work*," he scoffed. "I do it for fun. It relaxes me. But fun won't pay the bills. I need someone like you to manage my inventory. Ship my orders. Talk to customers when they're pissed off. You'll be a business consultant. By creating value for me, you'll create value for yourself."

I worked in Frick's living room on one of his many refurbished laptops while his kids jumped around and screamed at each other. He had boxes and boxes of items for sale, stacked against every wall and piled in every corner. A spare bedroom was converted into a warehouse. He also rented a storage unit across the street. Frick's wife, Katy, spent hours taking pictures for me to post online. My task was to research each item and write up a listing. Volume was key. The job could have easily been done by an AI but Frick wouldn't pay for one. Computer engineers were the worst middlemen of them all.

Most of Frick's time was spent on supply runs. He trolled thrift stores and block sales aplenty, but his real money-maker was a connection at his old additive manufacturing job. There were clients who liked to run up their credit, and when they spent too long in the red, a hold was placed on their account. Some clients never paid up, and the fulfillment center would be left holding a dozen gross of thermoplastic sex toys in the shape of a cartoon horse. Or whatever.

When something like that happened, Frick got a call.

When he wasn't acquiring stock or following up on cockamamie schemes, Frick would help me package orders. Sometimes, Katy fixed us a big dinner and we worked until midnight—it wasn't like I had anywhere better to be.

Sometimes, I dared to think that Frick and I could be friends.

He was a tightfisted old scrounger with all the compunctions of a hungry dog, but Frick was a prospector at heart. His efforts brought him chaff as often as wheat. What he loved more than anything else was finding a discarded rarity. An esoteric collector's item—unremarkable to the layman—but worth its weight in gold to the right buyer.

He encouraged me to do my own scrounging, even taught me how to look for certain treasures. He didn't pay much. Too little in fact to really live.

Sometimes, I created value for myself by losing a few of his items on the side. Never his newest acquisitions, which accumulated daily. Always something small, long-forgotten in the rat's nest he called a warehouse. The longer I worked for him, the better I became at stealing from him.

Frick's only real crime was believing he could get something for nothing.

—

The City's climate system was great at mimicking night and day, but not so much at mimicking seasons. Once a year, according to Anita, they injected nucleators into the air supply and dropped the temperature below freezing, creating an artificial storm of snow and ice that lasted the whole week of Saturnalia. The City became a winter wonderland. Everyone got the day off. It was great.

Or it used to be.

The tradition was vehemently opposed by special interest groups who claimed that snow season was unnecessarily burdensome for businesses. Such was their clout that Bastion City had briefly switched to a tropical model, but that too was abandoned when the monsoons drowned a famous local ostrich.

These days, the City had only one season: fog with intermittent rain. People advocated for a cool, dry ecosystem year-round, but that inevitably lead to questions about how they would pay for an overhaul to the ancient climate system. Not to mention what the League of Urban Ecological Conservationists and the Mycology Guild would have to say about changes to the humidity.

I didn't miss summers in the desert, nor had I ever cared much for snow, but I did miss the transitions between them. Bastion City was an entity in homeostasis. It never went to sleep. Never sped up or slowed down. It was always itself—a bright, wet, throbbing grind. People and events constantly colliding. There weren't any sunsets to separate one day from the next.

Nighttime consisted of soft, bluish light that was easy to ignore. You could trick yourself into thinking it was dark. But nothing mimicked the sun as it dipped below a mountain ridge, the sudden drop in temperature, the spikes of ambient color, or shadows in the slant of dusk.

You could get authentic Jovian food at any hour of the day. You could watch Sexmancers perform in Excelsior Park. You could join barhops and treasure hunts and pancake breakfasts and strange religions and drug-fueled orgies of the highest caliber. You could even meet a celebrity if you knew which restaurants were hot. And so much more.

You could get anything here.

But you couldn't have autumn air. Or sunsets. Or snow.

Chapter 5—We Now Return You to Castaway, Already in Progress

I dreamt I was in a bright, beautiful city, and had finally come home.

"Hey, Lenny, you awake? They called your number. Wake up."

I dozed fitfully, but could not ignore the stink of Dead Tomas' breath.

"You go ahead and take my spot," I said, still half asleep.

"You don't want it?" he asked.

"I'll get the next one."

Shifty Eyes Frank smacked me. "Get up, dammit. The Corporate Level needs its data entered."

"I'm not going to Corporate today," I said. "I'm getting a real assignment."

"Not if you don't show up for the interview."

I glared at him. "What're you doing here anyway? Don't you have a literal mountain of gold waiting for you at home?"

"Leonard, that was three months ago," said Shifty Eyes.

"The hell you say. Are you trying to gaslight me?"

"I'm serious. I paid off my gambling debts, bought a new liver, started a dog sanctuary, invested in REITs—your idea, by the way—and lost the rest on bug fights. I'm plumb outta cash."

"You're full of shit," I said. "We partied at The Lounge the other night. The night you came home from the Fly Level."

"We party at The Lounge all the time." Shifty Eyes gave me a piteous look with both of his eyes. "You've lost the thread, man. You need to get back to reality."

"I say again," came the voice over the PA. "Number eighty-one. Now helping number eighty-one. Get your ass up here, eighty-one."

Shifty Eyes resumed flipping through his magazine. "Quit screwing around, Leonard. You need this job."

I considered the possibility that Shifty Eyes wasn't fucking with me. Had it really been three months since the night he came back from the Fly Level?

If so, what had I been doing all this time?

I knew the answer, of course. I'd been going to the Corporate Level regularly. Like a drone. Five times a week or more.

I needed to go on a real adventure before I killed myself.

My interviewer arrived in a flurry of motion, stumbling gracelessly into the cubicle. She reeked of delicious scotch. She threw herself at her desk and giggled.

It was Anita Menard. Bright and beautiful.

"Hi, Leonard! It's me. Sorry I'm late—I forgot where I worked!" A mostly empty bottle of scotch appeared from under her desk and she poured two glasses. "I'm supposed to pretend that I don't know who you are, so let's keep things hush hush, eh? Don't wanna arouse suspicion."

"Uh, sure." I took the offered glass without hesitation. "It's nice to see you again, Ms. Menard."

"Don't even bother." She knocked her drink back. "Call me Anita."

"Alright, Anita." It felt good to say her first name so candidly. "I'm not used to seeing the same interviewer twice."

"Twice?" Her buzz evaporated. "How many times do you think we've interviewed, Leonard?"

"Uh, at least twice." I was off to a bad start. "Have you been in Castaway long?"

"Castaway? No. This is my first assignment on Level 1. Top secret stuff. But I've worked for the Guild a long, long time."

"Where're you from?"

She looked at me sadly. "Somewhere far away."

"Me too," I said, trying to sound reassuring. "I mean, we all are."

She looked even sadder.

"I'm sorry." I wasn't sure what I was apologizing for. "Maybe we should just get started?"

"Yes, let's do that." She rummaged through her desk for a pen and paper. "Let's get this crapshow on the road." Anita took a shot and wiped her mouth, lips glistening. "Tell me about you, sweetcheeks. Are you a hard worker? Driven? Ready to do whatever it takes?"

"Well," I said, gearing up, "I'm an independent thinker who follows instructions, but I always take risks without endangering—"

"Yeah-huh. And your skills? Could your skills conceivably pay the bills?"

"Uh, yes. I'm very adept at handling clerical matters. As an Expert Support Miscellaneous, my core proficiencies—"

"Superlative. And how do you feel about killing? Can you fight?"

This was not going well. "I'm not much of a killer. I do brain things. Not that it doesn't take intelligence to kill people, I suppose. I just mean that I'm not good at it. I'd like to be, I think."

"Good answer." Anita leaned forward in her chair. "Now for the real shit: what would you do to see your loved ones again?"

These were advanced questions—like none I'd ever been asked before. "Are you asking if I would allow my emotions to endanger the enterprise?"

"Love isn't an emotion. It's a statement of fact."

"Are you asking if I'm in love?"

"Are you?" Her eyes sparkled. "Are you patient and kind? Love certainly isn't. It's more like an alligator. Ancient. Remorseless."

I took a gulp of scotch. "I'm not like an alligator."

"I'm asking if you're true to your own nature. Like an alligator."

"Isn't everyone? That's the thing about nature. It can't help being what it is."

"You really don't remember me, do you?"

I was obviously in big trouble for something, but my brain wasn't working right. As I struggled to formulate an acceptable answer, Anita leaned further over the desk. Her blouse hung low.

My eyes shot towards the ceiling.

"Are you kidding me?"

"I thought I was being polite," I said.

"Look at my tits, dammit."

I glanced, and when she cleared her throat impatiently, I took a second, longer perusal. "They're good."

"Good?"

"Nice. They're…lovely."

"I know that." Her supermoon eyes were upon me. "That's not doing anything for you? Not jogging any memories?"

"I'm not sure what this is supposed to prove." I looked for a clue somewhere in the valley of her breasts. "Is it a test? Like an optical illusion?"

She sat back in her chair, sighing loudly.

"I'm not the type to get 'distracted' if that's what you're asking—"

"No, you gigantic dork." She took down her first notes. "Forget it."

"Look, I'm a professional. I've been doing this a long time now."

"And how long would that be?"

"Uh…years. At least a few years. Or more."

"Or more." Her gaze put a knife in my gut. "You can't give me an accurate figure? How long have you lived in Castaway?"

"Awhile, I guess? I never bothered to keep track."

"How did you come to this horrible place?"

"Like everyone else. The portal."

"Portal." She let the word linger on her tongue. "And where were you before you were portaled here? What were you doing?"

My glass was already empty. "I don't like that question."

"You don't remember me." Her voice was stone sober. "You don't remember anything, do you?"

I tried to offer a disarming grin but it felt like a rictus. "What does it matter when I was portaled or where I'm from? Castaway's my home now."

"No, it's not. This place is a tomb."

Why was she doing this to me? "I have my friends. I own a duplex. Life's not so bad."

"Could be better, though." She took more notes. "Could be much better."

"I know I've met you before," I said. "Before Castaway. I just don't remember how."

She suddenly looked on the verge of tears.

"I have a bad memory. I'm sorry."

"Leonard…" She huffed and wiped her eyes. "We do it to ourselves, this pain."

"Maybe I should go."

"Sit down," she commanded. "I have one last question. What does the name El Savel mean to you?"

I recoiled so hard I almost fell out of my chair.

"You've heard it before," she said.

"What the hell's going on?" I could feel a headache coming. "Why are you asking me these questions?"

"I'm a placement officer for the Adventurer's Guild."

"That's not what I meant. You asked me strange questions the first time we interviewed. A new HR process, you called it. What're you hiding?"

"You've no idea how much I wish I could tell you," she said with a sigh. "All of it. But both sides are watching, and if I tell you—if I just blurt it out—all of this will be for nothing. Just another iteration. It'll be nothing to them. The best I can do is give you an edge. Something the others don't have. So, answer the question, Mr. Marcs. You know who El

Savel is. The answer is inside you, just try to remember why. Think about where you came from."

"Stop it!" My brain was heating up. "Stop messing with my head."

"I'm not messing with your head, sweetcheeks."

"Bullshit. You liquor me up and you ask me all this crap about where I'm from and how long I've been an adventurer. You show me your…and El Savel? Who the fuck is El Savel?"

"That's the question." She folded her hands. "I would never mislead you, Leonard. You mean more to me than anyone."

I stepped out of the cubicle and shouted down to the vestibule. "Hello, could I get someone else to interview me? This one's defective."

I kept shouting until Anita yanked me back to the desk, her arms like iron bands around my chest.

"You want a job, don't you?" she hissed.

"Of course." Any ideas I had about fighting her dissolved as her fragrance wafted over me. "What perfume are you wearing?"

"That's not perfume." Her lips were next to my ear. "That's just me."

I could smell the scotch on her breath too. I liked it.

Her arms loosened, neither of us drawing away.

"It reminds me of a dream," I said, my hands quivering, longing for something that wasn't appropriate. "But everything feels like a dream these days. It takes a lot of work convincing myself that I'm real."

Her head pressed into my shoulder.

"Anita?"

"Yes, Lenny?"

"What happens after this moment passes?"

"That's up to you." She returned to her chair. "But I believe we have the perfect opening for you."

It was all a test. Another stupid test.

"A quest to Level 13," she continued. "The Bob Level."

I sat back down. "Not to be fussy, but I'm not sure an excursion to the Bob Level demands my skillset."

"What makes you say that?"

"I interpret clues, solve puzzles, read maps—that kind of thing. You don't find a lot of those obstacles on Level 13. Just monsters. And a town filled with Bobs. Thousands of copies of Bob trying to turn you into another copy of Bob."

She gazed at me for much longer than seemed professional.

Not that I minded.

"Level 13 is what I have available," she said finally. "The mission comes with an advance of twenty thousand. You keep twenty-five percent of the dosh."

My brain shat itself.

"The objective is to penetrate the City of Bobs, Omnidracogon, and to kill Bob Alpha."

I couldn't keep myself from laughing. "We already tried that. A little thing called the Massacre on Level 13."

"Wolfram Selma killed Bob Alpha all by herself and she was just a girl."

"Wolfram Selma was a legend. She was also the only one in her party that made it home alive. Who's commissioning this thing?"

"You know I can't tell you that."

"But is it the same guys who commissioned the last attempt?"

"The people financing this quest understand its importance, and they understand what it requires. Getting rid of Bob Alpha is only the first objective. The second is to recover his heart and bring it to Castaway intact."

I laughed again. "Even Wolfram Selma couldn't manage that. The Alpha's heart is just a myth as far as anyone knows."

"We're not asking for miracles, just results." All traces of Anita's former warmth and familiarity were gone. "Compensation for achieving this secondary objective is far more generous. Each member of your party will be granted one million preferred shares of the Adventurer's Guild Financial Trust. At current NAV, the equity would be worth over seventy-two million. This income would represent a capital gain not subject to Guild dues."

My brain shat itself again, then rolled in the shit.

"What do you think, Mr. Marcs? Is that acceptable to you?"

I wanted to leap over the desk and kiss her. "How can I say no?"

She looked, for a moment, fearful that I might.

I put on what I thought was a mischievous smile. "I'm going out with some friends tonight. Wanna come?"

"Nothing would make me happier." Anita took a long pull of scotch right from the bottle and slammed it on the desk, slouching insouciantly in her chair. "But I've got a lot of work to do."

I looked meaningfully at the booze and then at the lack of booze in my glass.

"I need your answer now," she said.

"I'll take the job," I replied.

"Good." She snatched the bottle away and left the cubicle.

—

Shifty Eyes, Dead Tomas, Ron, the Mighty Minotaur, Skeleton Wendy, Akk Akk from the deli, Orlando, and I all met at the Red Dog that evening for a pint of expired mana potion. Doing so offered the mind a short jaunt through the depths of the Æther—the cheapest high on the market.

"I can't believe we all got the same quest," said Shifty Eyes, swirling the blue-purple concoction in his glass. "It sounds like a conspiracy."

Ron downed his potion. "After what happened last time I wouldn't be surprised if they hired half the town."

"But who could afford something like that?" asked Dead Tomas.

"Here's the better question," said Ron, eyes glowing with light. "How valuable is the heart of Bob Alpha?"

"Obviously pretty damn valuable," said Shifty Eyes. "But since no one's ever gotten the heart, we don't know what it does."

The Mighty Minotaur roared for more mana potion, already winking in and out of existence.

"But can you believe the jackpot?" I said. "Think of what we could do with that kind of financial independence."

"The compensation is a ruse," said Shifty Eyes, still sipping his mana potion. "It's a suicide mission. They hardly expect anyone to come back."

"But you took the job," I said.

"Fuck yeah I took the job," he replied.

I started to lift off the ground.

"Tell me something, Leonard." Shifty Eyes was being unusually circumspect today. "Did you ask her why?"

"Who?" I asked.

"The interviewer," he replied impatiently. "Anita."

"I didn't have to." My head filled with secrets. "She was just fucking with me. She was cute, though. I can't believe I forgot a face like that."

"No, idiot," said Shifty Eyes. "I meant why did she pick you, of all people, for the mission?"

I was stung.

"Come off it, Leonard. Your goose is cooked on Level 13. It's nothing but wave after wave of elites. And once you're done with them, you gotta deal with the Bobs. There's no finessing the Bobs."

"Yeah, I know." My words bounced off his head and floated away. "That's what I told her."

"And?" Shifty Eyes had a major bug up his butt. "We're talking about the most difficult quest in Castaway's history. What skills does an Expert Support Miscellaneous possess that would make you an asset to this incredibly stupid enterprise?"

"She must have had her reasons," I muttered.

Shifty Eyes swallowed his mana potion. "You know what I think? I think these fuckers are out to get you."

"Not this again," said Ron from up in the rafters.

"He's been acting way weirder than usual," argued Shifty Eyes. "I don't think any of this is just a coincidence."

"You don't know what you're talking about," said my corporeal form, now an island on the horizon. "You don't know anything at all."

"Exactly." Shifty Eyes settled into a wooden statue of himself, groaning and creaking. "It's driving me nuts. What happened with that fish you found on your door? That's all you could talk about for weeks. Guys in black armor. Dude in an alligator costume. You were waving that stupid candy gun around, saying you were gonna have a chat with the Fishmancers. And now? It's like you don't even remember it."

"I *don't* remember it," I shouted. "Let it go. I'm trying to get high."

Shifty Eyes became a distant echo. "I want answers, Leonard."

"Answers." A lightbulb went on in my skull, hauling me from the undertow of pleasure and back into the bar. "Oh shit, I never heard back from Araxi. She was supposed to ask around about the Mana Fish. See if people were robbing Fishmancers or something."

Shifty Eyes looked sick to his stomach. "Leonard, no one's seen Araxi in months. Not since you visited her shop."

A pair of alligator jaws lurked in my peripheral vision, remaining just out of sight no matter which way I turned.

Shifty Eyes shook his head. "You have to make this right."

"I know," I said, bobbing listlessly along the floor. "Goddammit."

"Stop sulking and get up here," said Ron's disembodied voice from the Æther. "Dead Tomas is now Alive Tomas and he's shockingly handsome."

Shifty Eyes took my hand and we floated away together.

And though Dead Tomas was shockingly handsome, as were all of us, beautiful and immortal in the Ætheric Gardens beyond all reason and flesh, I could not forget those alligator jaws, for the Alligator had not forgotten me.

It knew what I'd done.

—

My yard collapsed into a sinkhole the moment I started digging. Solid dirt transformed into a cavern of mud. I combed through it, looking for the Mana Fish. I eventually found it by wrapping my fingers around the dagger's blade and slicing them to the bone.

I squeezed my wrist and the arteries within, clenching my teeth like I could force the pain out through my ears. Mud sloughed away as gouts of blood pooled on my palm. I was gonna need a healer.

All at once, the pain vanished. Blood slowed to a trickle, then reversed, flowing backwards into my wounds and sealing them up. The lacerations vanished, leaving raised lines of angry flesh that soon disappeared as well.

The skin wasn't even tender.

"That's pretty weird," I said to no one.

I put the fish and dagger in a large casserole dish I never used, wrapped them in tinfoil, and stuck them in my adventuring bag. I loaded the bubblegum special and grabbed my briefcase full of money.

On my way to Araxi's Pawn & Gun, no less than ten people slalomed out of the portal, each one crazier and more naked than the last. Armed too. They rattled sabers and maces and flails of bone, their bodies painted red and white, a cloud of flies surrounding them.

Their twin leaders were conjoined at the shoulder and hip, wielding a hand-and-a-half sword each, heavy bands of gold around their arms, masks of gilded leaves twined with red roses in bloom.

They spoke with one voice. "The Order of the Sublime Reliquary comes to you, Castaway, for there is a debt that must be paid. A wrong that shall be righted. El Savel has taken that which does not belong to him and has hidden it where he thinks we cannot go. But we go where we want, Castaway. You will cooperate, or you will face death. Death, we say! Death for all of you."

Someone looked up from his large, uncooperative hoagie. "Did those naked conjoined twins say something about death?"

"Death!" they reaffirmed, and smote the sandwich-eater with a ray of blinding light.

Surrounding the portal, the Munis wasted no time opening fire.

The cultists were strong—their bodies filled with a holy hatred that deflected laser blasts—but their magical rage could only take so much.

They were soon outgunned.

"Damn you, El Savel," cried the twins, their roses erupting in flames as they were shot to mush. "You will pay for your arrogance! You. Will. Pay."

Their final words echoed in Central Plaza long after they

disintegrated.

I hurried onward to Araxi's Pawn & Gun before the Munis could detain everyone for questioning. The shop was packed. They hadn't kept up with the frankincense, leaving the air polluted with the stench of unwashed adventurers. I elbowed my way through the crowd, determined, but uncertain about who or what I was looking for.

"Well goodness-fucking-gracious," said a voice right next to me. "Look who finally showed up."

It took me a moment to realize I was being admonished by Rolla and not a large, agitated dumpling. No longer sitting behind the power gauntlet display, the old pug woman stood a head shorter than me, her chocolate eyes full of malice.

"You're the fucko with the fish," she said.

"The name's Leonard," I replied, holding out a hand.

"Your name's Fartface O'Houlihan as far as I'm concerned." She slapped my hand away and jabbed me in the chest. "You got Araxi into a world of trouble with that fish nonsense. And now you're gonna get her out of it. Follow me."

Rolla led me behind the counter, which felt transgressive. She opened a secret passageway that took us through a stockroom, through a freezer, under the legs of two giants holding scimitars, and finally, to the Back of the Store, a liminal space that connected every shop in Castaway. Only Muni traders and other elite members of society were permitted back here.

What a roller coaster of a day this was turning into.

Massive metal shelves rose seventy feet high, loaded with barrels, boxes, hogsheads, and pallets of every imaginable commodity. Reach trucks zipped in and out of the labyrinth, their drivers honking wildly, swerving at every intersection to avoid hitting one another. The cavernous space amplified every voice and footstep. From somewhere deep in the bowels of the warehouse came the sounds of power tools, smashing pallets, and stranger things yet.

"This place is amazing," I said.

"It's just a regional cost center," said Rolla. "You should see our Bastion City location."

"Which Level is that on?"

She made an oinking sound that I interpreted as laughter.

Arriving at the main desk, she seated herself behind a terminal. Several warehouse workers loitered nearby, smoking cigarettes and eating cheese fries, barely glancing at us. Rolla snorted laboriously as her furry little fingers stabbed at the keyboard.

Her ears looked velvety soft and I had an urge to pet them.

An image popped up on the terminal: a blown-up picture of my face the day I came to Castaway. It was the same mugshot I carried around on my Guild license and Municipal Co-op card.

"Your profile," she said, her chops turned up in a smirk. "I have admin privileges too. Wanna see me change your name?"

"No thank you," I said.

I was renamed Ernest Bumwaller.

"I can change anything," she said. "How much do you weigh?"

"Look, I came to help Araxi."

"Ninety days late."

I squirmed under the weight of that number. "Just tell me what happened."

Rolla folded her arms, which sank into her voluminous folds. "Araxi went to the aquarium store for answers. It should have been a quick visit, but we never saw her again. They eventually sent us a ransom note."

"Seriously? What the hell's their problem?"

"The Circle of Magi is desperate for leverage. Not only is someone stealing their Mana Fish, they're dropping mancers left and right. Ambushing people on quests. Killing them in magical opium dens."

"I've never heard anything about this," I said, amazed.

"Of course not. You don't know shit from shoe polish, Leonard Marcs."

"So how come you didn't pay the ransom?"

"Because we don't negotiate with terrorists," grunted Rolla. "But that doesn't mean we won't do whatever needs doin' to get our agent back."

"Araxi is one of your agents?"

"Yes, you great cretin. Pay attention. Her pawnshop is just a cover. She really works for us."

"Right…and who are you, again?"

Rolla gave me a withering look. "We're the fucking Pan-Dimensional Services Commission."

"Oh shit," I said. "I thought the Munis owned the Guild."

"So what? We own the Levels. We built this place."

I stalled, trying to put all the pieces together in my head and coming up short. "If you are who you say you are, why do you need my help?"

Rolla pulled a donut out of a hidden pouch and started munching. "Even if the Pan-Dimensional Services Commission had an extralegal fighting force that could perform a daring rescue mission—which it doesn't—it would mean the Hero Wars all over again. The Circle of Magi is not our real enemy. We need an Expert like you to *finesse* the situation. That's how you adventurers talk, right?"

"Uh, sure." My head was spinning. "But what exactly do you want me to do? I can't just walk up to the Fishmancers and demand they release Araxi."

"You're the Expert, poopslice. Figure out the details. Do whatever it is you do when faced with an obstacle that can't be overcome by force. And if you can't do that, at least have the decency to die trying."

"Do I need to contact the Guild, or are we doing this under the table?"

Rolla choked on her donut. "This is on your dime, pally. You're the one who got Araxi in trouble."

"Not completely. You sent one of your agents to the aquarium store, alone, without any field intelligence. Even the Guild's not that sloppy."

Rolla's hackles went up. "You're getting between me and my human. Is that what you want? Because that's a good way to lose your head."

I shrugged in defiance. "I'll just go home if you won't tell me the truth."

For once, the look on her face was not one of smirking contempt. "You called my bluff, human. The truth is that Araxi is just a freelancer. A prole like you. The Commission has a strict non-interference policy when it comes to internecine conflicts, so my bosses don't give two shits whether she lives or dies. I filed for an exemption but was denied. Guilting you is my only option."

"Okay, that makes more sense." I stroked my chin to show her I was thinking. "What I don't understand is why Araxi went to the aquarium store at all. I thought she had contacts. People she could tap for information."

"I'm also curious as to why she stuck her neck out for someone so appallingly ignorant. Were you two sleeping together?"

"Not that it's any of your business, pug, but neither of us were interested. She's like a cousin to me."

"Uh huh," said Rolla, her giant black dog eyes casting aspersions left, right, and center. "You tried."

"You got me figured wrong. I buried that part of myself a long time ago."

Rolla snorted. "There's something wrong with you, Bumwaller."

"Could you please change my name back to Leonard?"

"I'm looking right at you, but my nose tells me you're not really there. You smell like the *traces* of a person. Like a blood trail in some bigger, stupider mystery. And you've got a vacant-eyed look plastered over that idiot face of yours. I can't even tell if you're paying attention to me right now. It's unnerving. How does anyone put up with you?"

"Araxi put up with me," I said.

"And look where that got her."

I nodded miserably. "I'll help. For free."

"Thank you for the bare minimum of decency." Rolla changed everything with a few keystrokes. "Congratulations, Leonard Marcs, you've been re-designated a Fishmancer."

"What?" That was not what I had in mind. "But…why?"

"That's how you'll get into the aquarium store."

"But I don't know the first thing about magic."

"You've got a Mana Fish," said Rolla with an affable wink. "You've got a big trench coat. What else do you need? Use your razor-sharp wit. Find out where they're keeping my human. I don't wanna see your fucking face until you know something useful."

I stroked my chin at her.

"What the fuck are you staring at?" she demanded.

"There's something you're not telling me," I said.

She reclined in her chair. "There's a lot of stuff I'm not telling you. About you. About the fish on your door. Information is the most valuable commodity in the Multiverse. But if you bring my human back, I'll tell you what I know. Perhaps I'll even tell you about that lovely, young-ish woman at the Guild with the rhinestone eyes. Anita. I'm sure you're dying to know about her."

My cheeks flamed.

"Or don't you want her either?" Rolla taunted.

"How can I trust you?"

"Oh, that's the easy part." Rolla pulled out a dagger, blacker than sin. "We're gonna make a pact. There's power in the blood, and it will bind us to the Way of Truth. Give me your hand."

"The Pan-Dimensional Services Commission practices magic?"

"We practice everything."

As she sliced our palms, something stirred within me. Was it the remnants of the expired mana potion? It felt familiar. Another promise I made long ago. Another blood pact. Nearly forgotten.

When the blood started to flow, all I could see were teeth.

—

I waited at the Guild for hours.

I didn't have a plan. I didn't even know what I wanted to tell her. But I needed to see Anita. Was I warning her? Was I stalking her? Did I think she had answers? I had to see those magnificent eyes again. Maybe drink her scotch.

I should have brought a gift.

After many, many numbers were called up, I was personally escorted to a placement officer who was definitely not Anita. It was a doughy, inoffensive pencil-pusher named Ernie B.

"I'm sorry, but Ms. Menard isn't in today," he said while taking detailed notes. "She's got a bad case of scurvy."

"Scurvy?" I said. "That's not a thing."

"It most certainly is! Lots of people get scurvy. Not enough oranges in their diet. Have you ever heard of the Orange Bandits? They robbed banks while sucking on orange peels. Made it look like they had fake plastic mouths. No teeth. Cuz of scurvy. Super off-putting."

"I find this all very difficult to believe, Ernie."

Ernie pounded his desk. "Hey, pal, we don't even know each other. You call me Mr. Belfour. Does that make sense to you?"

"I need to speak to Anita. Can you tell me where she lives?"

"I can't give out information like that! It's against Guild regulations. And highly unprofessional."

"Alright," I said, thinking fast. "What does she do for fun?"

"What in heaven's name are you talking about? I thought you wanted to know where she lives."

"I do. But you said you won't tell me."

"That's correct."

"And she's off duty?

"Alita is taking a personal day, yes."

"You mean Anita."

"Right."

"So maybe she's doing something recreational. Just give me a hint."

"I told you she was sick."

"Yeah, but I didn't believe you," I said.

Ernie sighed. "Mr. Marcs, telling you what she does for fun would be just as inappropriate as telling you where she lives. Imagine if you were looking for me, instead of Anita, and you asked her—instead of me—where I was and what I did in my spare time. Imagine if you asked whether my wife—Breanne Belfour—and I were open to the possibility of having a threesome. That would be crazy."

"How about you give me a statistically-based answer? Nothing definite. A 50% chance, let's say, that Anita enjoys karaoke. I could work with that."

Ernie glowered. "I'd say there's a 0% chance I'm gonna help you stalk one of my coworkers."

"I'm not stalking," I protested. "I'm following up."

"This line of inquiry is fruitless, Mr. Marcs. I don't condone fraternization with Guild contractors. Unless…how do you feel about swingers? Any experience there?"

"What if I told you she was in trouble?" I said, trying to prevent myself from reaching over the desk and strangling him.

"My wife?" asked Ernie, alarmed.

"Anita," I clarified.

"And trouble with a capital 'T,' you might say?"

"I wouldn't."

"Well, if that's the case, Mr. Marcs, you should leave a detailed statement specifying the exact nature of your nebulous suspicions. We could followup later. Perhaps over a drink. Breanne gets off at five."

"Listen, Belfour." I stood up and did my best to look menacing. "I don't want to leave a detailed message, and I don't want to fuck your wife. My only concern is Anita."

Ernie reached unsubtly beneath his desk. "I think the person you should be concerned with is yourself, Mr. Marcs. You're wading into territory well beyond your limited acumen."

"You don't even know who Anita is, do you?"

"It would be wise to submit yourself to Guild custody, Mr. Marcs. Just a formality, you understand. Just until we can get a handle on the situation and be sure that Amanda is safe. Does that suit you?"

It didn't suit me at all.

Ernie raised his gun and I swung my briefcase. Jangling with heavy coinage and bars of precious metals, it connected with his temple and laid him out cold on the office floor. His eyes were stuck open, his doughy face slack. His gun was just a wooden prop.

The silent alarm on the underside of his desk was not.

Someone came at me from behind, spun me around.

Fortunately, the assailant kissed me rather than murder me.

"Lenny," she said, touching my face.

"Anita," I replied, my hands in her hair, on her shoulders, caressing her cheeks. "What's happening?"

"I can't tell you," she said, holding me close. "You're almost where you need to be. Get to the aquarium store while there's still time."

"You're in danger," I said, breathless. "This pug, she knows something. And the Pan-Dimensional Services Commission. And the

Fishmancers. I don't know what it means—"

She kissed me again, silencing my ramble.

"Will you be alright?" I asked.

She nodded. "I'm leaving town. You need to go."

I cried, but didn't know why. "Will I see you again?"

She stifled a sob and wiped one of my cheeks. "I hope so."

I ran from the cubicle farm as fast as I could, trailing a conga line of office personnel. They waved their fake guns and demanded that I stop in the name of love. I yanked fistfuls of money out of my briefcase and lobbed them over my shoulder as I vaulted down the hill at breakneck speed.

Some took the money. Others were foolish enough to pursue. One lost his balance and stumbled into his coworker, starting a chain reaction that led to an avalanche of rolling bureaucrats.

I hit the bottom and kept running.

The mass of bureaucrats struck the ground like a pile of tangled Slinkies, their bones snapping audibly on the pavement. I turned a corner and disappeared into downtown Castaway.

Chapter 6—The Joys of Shopping

Desmond's Donuts had the brightest, most obnoxious lights of any business in the old Piggy Bank District. Its signage depicted a green iguana chomping into a big, pink donut, but the iguana's bite left no mark upon the confection. With a flash and a sizzle, the lizard opened its mouth for another chomp, and the donut reconstituted itself.

I often wondered if Desmond, the donut-loving iguana, was meant to be a glutton or a victim. Was he merely the donut's opposite? An insatiable force pitted against an everlasting object? Or was this the lizard's torment? Had some monstrous force condemned him to an impossible task? The owner did not answer my queries regarding the matter.

Amidst the panoply of colors, especially at night, it was easy to overlook Desmond's neighbor, a sandstone building with a rudimentary white and black sign. Exotic Aquatics. The unremarkable exterior belied the shop's importance. The "secret" headquarters for every Fishmancer on Level 1.

A door chime heralded my entrance but no one came to greet me.

The stink of foul carpet permeated the air. Water condensed on yellowed walls and rusted shelves, haphazardly stocked with fish food and potions. Empty glass aquariums littered the floor, some of them stacked on display, others broken and covered in cobwebs.

Where were all the fish?

"Hello?" I called. "New Fishmancer here. Need some help."

No one responded. The Mana Fish turned my pockets into waterfalls.

I followed the serpentine pattern of the store. With each corner I rounded, the lights grew dimmer, the floor damper, and the smell of putrefaction intensified. The hum and bubble of aquaculture was omnipresent, but not a single fish tank came into view. No store clerks. No wizards. Just roaches and mold.

I held the Mana Fish aloft as tightly as I could while clutching my briefcase between my knees. "Make with me a covenant, mighty Fishmancers," I intoned. "I'll be yours if you'll be mine."

Everything went still. Cavitation ceased. Roaches froze and bulbs stopped flickering. I could hear the carpet rot.

From behind a secret door, someone finally emerged.

They were dressed in an atmospheric diving suit of ancient and draconian design. Without the buoyancy of water to hold it, each of the diver's steps was an agonizing trudge. A colossal entity, impossibly large in that tiny shop. The floor popped under its weight. The porthole of its dingy copper helmet shone with a light that obscured its face, and it spoke in a dissonant machine language, an electric shrieking not intended for human ears.

The diver trained its headlamp on the Mana Fish in my hands.

It stared for a long time.

The diver raised a hand the size of a picnic ham and twisted a valve on the side of its helmet. Water jets erupted from tiny cracks around the porthole, widening with each twist of the valve. The store flooded. I stuffed the Mana Fish back in my coat and grabbed my briefcase. With a final twist, the porthole snapped open, releasing a tidal wave that swept me off my feet.

I didn't know which direction was up. I expected to break my head on the floor but tumbled through open water instead.

Momentum slowed. I opened my eyes.

Gone was the decaying shop, replaced by an ocean. The ceiling was a distant tarp of shimmering light. The diver and I floated within a massive aquarium.

"Can you understand me now?" Underwater, the diver's horrible language became a soft, androgynous voice.

I gesticulated, concerned with air.

"It's magic, sir. Just breathe normally."

Swallowing a lungful of seawater was excruciating at first, but the shock wore off and I was able to breathe again.

"My name is Jarc," said the diver.

"Hi, there." My voice projected oddly. "I'm new."

"Yes," agreed Jarc.

"In fact, I was designated a Fishmancer today, and I could use some help."

The Mana Fish—escaped in the deluge—returned with a vengeance to ram me with its sharp, boney body.

"I could use some help," I repeated, trying to protect my face while the Mana Fish inflicted blow after blow. "Please. Oh god. Please help me."

Jarc whistled and the fish broke off its assault.

"This creature isn't bound to you." Jarc was able to calm the Mana Fish, which began orbiting the diver's helmet lazily. "Her emotions are murky, full of desperation and pain. Have you abused her?"

Guilt spiked in my guts. "She was left on my doorstep."

"A regrettable but not uncommon occurrence. Some find the demands of the Covenant too difficult to bear. But one mancer's dereliction summons another to our ranks. What do you find attractive about the arcane?"

"Gosh," I said. "Everything? Who doesn't want to use magic?"

"Few are prepared for the responsibility. Fewer still can earn a place within the Circle. We have a rigorous training process that demands years of dedication. A lifetime to master."

"Oh," I said. "Well, I don't have time for that."

Jarc chuckled. "Then there's little I can do for you, newly-designated one. Fishmancy is more than a trade. It is a path to enlightenment. Everything came from the Infinite Ocean, and everything will eventually return. The Sublime Garden is the dwelling-place of only the most fervent disciples."

"Look, we can worry about divine mysteries later. I just need enough tutelage to get me started on this quest. Even mancers gotta pay the bills, right?"

Jarc gazed at the shimmering ceiling. "If you join our ranks, you will face unimaginable peril. The less 'tutelage' you receive, the more likely you are to perish."

"There's got to be something you can do for me."

"Indeed." Jarc contemplated me. "There is a technique which may—without the benefit of formal training—convert a layman into a full mancer. Such an avenue is dangerous, irresponsible…and expensive."

"I brought you the Mana Fish. Shouldn't that cover it?"

The diver chuckled. "She was never yours to give."

I carefully opened my briefcase, allowing Jarc a glimpse inside without letting the bills float away. "What do you take?"

Jarc chuckled again. "Now I see. You want to buy your way into a better Designation."

My ears burned. "It's not like that."

"It's no business of mine, newly-designated one. I won't ask how you acquired her, but if this Mana Fish was poached, I will know the truth of it sooner or later." Jarc snatched away my briefcase. "In the meantime, let me introduce you to our walk-in tutor, Longinus bin Hashim. You will meet him shortly."

Jarc shoved me and I was picked up by a strong and sudden current.

"I'm gonna need that briefcase back," I shouted.

The current carried me over a murky desert. Perfect white dunes of sand passed underneath, continuing for miles until a jagged ridge of rock loomed out of the water. The current took me downward, and the ridge split into a ravine.

Mounds of coral grew in a forest of pillared, iridescent thorns. Sea anemones trailed fat tentacles amid kelp fields and spires of rock covered in the razor lips of oysters. Electric scallops pulsed. Dendritic polyps clenched and unclenched like hands in greeting as I passed. Nervous neon fish picked at the sand, scattered at the slightest provocation, and regrouped with effortless grace.

The current brought me to a statue encrusted with barnacles, its face obscured by generations of algae. I grabbed at its slimy, outstretched hands, trying to prevent myself from being keelhauled on its chest.

"Welcome to the Garden," said the statue in a somber, masculine tone. "I am the one called Longinus bin Hashim."

The current ebbed and I was able to regain my footing. "That diver, Jarc, took my briefcase."

"They tell me you wish to learn the ways of the Covenant," said Longinus, his stone lips immobile, "and that you have a great need for expediency."

"Uh, yeah, you could say that."

"By what name do they call you?"

"…Marcus."

"Very well. Tell me about yourself, Marcus, and what you hope to gain from the arcane arts."

"Power? I'm hoping for power."

"I enjoy your candor, Marcus, but I was actually inquiring about your spiritual desires."

"Before we get to all that," I said, trying to sound circumspect, "maybe you can do me a favor."

"A favor? So early in our acquaintance? That is quite bold."

"I'm looking for a friend of mine. She visited about three months ago, I think. Black hair, three eyeballs, wears a lot of tight leather. It sounds tacky but she makes it work. Have you seen her?"

"What does that have to do with your training?" asked Longinus after an uncomfortable pause.

"Uh, she owes me money. A lot of money. Lost a bet on the bug fights. You know how it is."

"I see," said Longinus. "Let's take a walk."

We bounced along the ravine floor, the Garden growing brighter and more elaborate. Corals and sponges matted the sand like decorative rugs, traversed in the millions by urchins and snails and nudibranchs displaying a wealth of colorful geometries. Seahorses clung to coral branches and juts of rock, their tiny fins barely keeping them upright. Angelfish and anemonefish and flatfish darted between hiding spots, slunk underfoot, and inspected our clothing.

"Ours is the Circle that Bends," explained Longinus. "The way of life—the water element. Most similar to us are the Fungusmancers and Birdmancers, for they too channel the mysteries of living arcana. Most dissimilar to us are the Dinnermancers, Sexmancers, and Cartomancers, for they lack conviction, believing only in ritual and gaudy miracles. And the Candymakers? They are hardly mancers at all. More like technicians. Skilled at wringing magic from artifice, but little else. Theirs is the Circle that Terminates. A dead end. We have always vied with our cousins for supremacy, but this new enemy defies understanding. You wouldn't believe the things they have done to us."

Seaweed formed a canopy. Corals gave way to rocks that glowed like moonlit marble. Longinus took my hand and guided me into the dark. We were inside the reef now. Blood roared in my eardrums.

"There are many kinds of mancy, but only two kinds of magic," continued Longinus, his voice amplified. "Invocation calls upon forces greater than ourselves. For a price. Evocation comes from within. The majority of our disciples must train for years, accumulating great knowledge and power, before they can bond with a familiar. But there are individuals for whom this power is already present within them. A birthright or some unknown providence. These individuals are exceedingly rare, but if you are such an individual, a familiar will make with you a Covenant as readily as a child bonds to its caregiver."

"And that will train me to be a mancer?"

Longinus let go of my hand and I scrabbled in the darkness.

"What's happening?" I asked. "Where've you gone?"

"This 'friend' of yours, she had unwelcome questions. You are much the same, Leonard Marcs. So here is the one and only way you will make it out of this place alive. Prove to me your worth."

"She was just trying to do me a favor, Longinus. Let her go."

"Form a Covenant or die."
"And give me back my briefcase full of money!"
I tried to grab him, but Longinus had gone.
Fuck Fishmancy.

Chapter 7—A Beautiful Friendship

I was determined, apparently, to hit every sharp rock I could find as I bumbled through the darkness of the under-reef. The stagnant water filled with the scent of my blood.

Hours had passed since Longinus trapped me.

I tried to avoid thinking of all the nested levels of claustrophobia in which I was immersed. Under a rock. Under an ocean. Hidden in a moldy fish shop. Forgotten at the lowest of Level of the Multiverse.

Horrible things lived at these depths.

Rumination lived here. Rumination awaited me in the darkness, had waited this whole time, knew it would find me, and did.

Every day in Castaway was a blur, each mission a dream, each year dissolved into the one before it. My head was an endless, hollow space for memories.

All things could be forgotten in that vast interior.

Had I any goals when I arrived in Castaway? They were lost to me now, hidden behind barriers of my own design. I could learn not to mind if I could learn how to forget that I had forgotten. But each omission was another layer of abstraction in my brain, another level in the stack of nightmares I would have to claw through if I wanted escape.

And I could not stop wanting an escape from this world. This career.

Who even was I anymore?

For a second, I thought I'd stumbled onto a giant, outstretched tongue.

Something slimy and soft.

The tongue bit me.

Hundreds of glass shards pierced my flesh, spread up my arm and over my chest. I tried to yank the tongue away and it filled my hands with barbs. It flexed its muscles, wrapped around my neck, and choked me into submission. The tongue kept stinging, using larger and larger barbs. They pierced my cheeks and went into my throat. They impaled my eyes right through the lids.

My veins filled with venom. I wanted to scratch myself open.

The tongue was on my scalp, threading needles in my hair. It flopped down on my face and pressed its slimy bulk to my nose.

The tongue was a worm, its head covered in fine tufts of calcareous bristles.

The tufts quivered on my cheeks. Like cat whiskers.

Would that I could scream.

The giant rockworm had me under its control. It had no words, but it had plans. I belonged to the worm, now, and I would do as it told me.

The worm bade me crawl through its tunnels into the heart of the reef. Walls so tight the barbs broke off in my flesh and burrowed their way to the bone.

I was blind and mute. Muscles full of poisoned glass.

The worm could have my body. But it couldn't have my mind.

What was up with that stupid movie Dead Tomas made me watch? The fight scene where the guy battles his own reflection. It wasn't a reflection, but a clone. Or a copy living inside a mirror. The copy wanted to stay hidden in that mirror, but it also wanted to be real. Both reflection and viewer.

A malevolent simulacrum. A doppelganger.

The constriction of the rockworm became a chokehold—someone with their arms and legs wrapped around my body.

Just like the protagonist being suffocated by his own reflection.

Me suffocating me. I couldn't let me get in the way of my own plans. I would not be abandoned at the bottom of the world.

Angry vomit gushed from my perforated mouth.

The worm fought to subdue me again, but I was already filled with needles. It couldn't hurt me more than it already had. I sunk my nails deep into its slimy flesh and pulled it apart, segment by segment, ripping it from my face.

With each agonizing detachment, I grew stronger.

Crazier.

The worm gave up trying to dominate and coiled into a ball of defensive spikes.

It begged for mercy.

I showed it none.

I pried and strangled and groped, tearing at the worm's bristles until it was defenseless. I bit into its body cavity and tore out its organs.

We thrashed in the bowels of the earth together until the worm was nothing.

I didn't know where I was going, but I twisted through crevices and cracks and narrow tunnels until I hit open water.

At last, I yanked the barbs from my eyes.

I was in a cavern of light. The walls were covered top to bottom in disc anemones and Saturnalia tree worms, emitting soft, azure and pink lights. A beautiful oasis, but a dead end. There were no more tunnels. Just the fissure through which I'd barely escaped.

I was delirious with venom. Death was surely imminent.

—

It was soon apparent the cavern had a bad case of eels. I tried to die in peace, but they darted out from tiny openings in the wall to eat the remnants of the worm, and when they were finished eating, they began to ram me with their little bodies. They were smaller than garden snakes, but surprisingly forceful. One of them wiggled under my nose and tickled me.

The little bastards were fast.

I demanded answers. What could a colony of eels want from me?

"They wanna know what's got you blue," said a kind and melodious voice.

The fattest eel of them all emerged. Its graceful, lemon and teal body was offset by a pair of unblinking googly eyes. Its mouth hung gormlessly open, like it was anticipating a joke. It was easily the most preposterous creature I'd ever encountered.

"C'mon," said the eel. "Tell ol' Heavenly Bogo what's got you in a funk."

"I don't think it would interest you much," I said.

"Why's that?"

"With a name like Heavenly Bogo, I assume you're magic."

"Very."

"A timeless and unfathomable creature from beyond this world."

"Flatterer."

"My problems wouldn't interest you."

"I asked, didn't I? C'mon, what's your name?"

"Leonard Marcs."

A group of eels nudged my side and began rolling me in the water.

It was gentle. Relaxing.

"It's a nice name," said Heavenly Bogo. "Tell me more."

I sighed. "Well, it's like this: I think I'm gonna die. I was attacked by a spikey rockworm and it got me bad."

"That's nasty."

"I thought—for some reason—that I might not be able to die. I don't know why, it's just a feeling I've always had. I never took it seriously, but now that I'm actually dying, I'm pretty disappointed. I'd hoped I was special. Like there was something important I needed to do. It doesn't matter now. Look at me. I'm definitely dying."

"Don't be too hard on yourself." Heavenly Bogo inspected me with its fishy nostrils. "You appear to be filled with a network of molecular biomachines that are operating off Ætherium energy. They can synthesize any molecule your body would ever need, which is pretty rad. In fact, they're repairing your body now as we speak."

"Really? That's amazing."

"I'm surprised you forgot you had those."

"There's a lot of important stuff I don't remember."

"I wouldn't say you're immortal, though. These machines are using up a lot of bandwidth. Synthesizing molecules out of Æther costs beaucoup bucks."

"I've never received a bill."

"Then someone must be looking out for you."

"So, I'm not dying. I'm gonna be okay."

"Yes, but you don't seem happy about it."

The itchiness in my blood diminished and my head no longer felt like it was on fire. I wanted a drink.

"Can we get real for a second, Leonard?" The eel cuddled up close. "You're not afraid of death. What's really going on? Sock it to me."

I lost myself in Heavenly Bogo's inconspicuous eyes—it felt like the eel and I were old friends. "I was sent here to find someone in the Garden. And before that, I was sent to Castaway to find an artifact. I think. People come to Castaway by accident, or are forced here, but not me. I had a mission. I don't like to think about it because I can't remember what it was. Now that I'm trapped here, it's all I can think about, and if I think too hard, I get this feeling like I might disintegrate."

Heavenly Bogo stared at me. Fish don't have expressions, but Heavenly Bogo had one. An expression of sweetness. Could eels be sweet?

"Listen to me, Leonard. You're going about this thing all wrong. You think you've got to open the right door? Walk the right path? Be the right sort of guy?"

"Yeah. Yeah, you get it."

"There are no paths, Leonard, let alone a single correct path that will make you happy. Nothing ever needs to be anything, which is why it's amazing that anything exists at all. Fear is a natural response to existence, and we are conditioned to respond to our fears because they are usually telling us something important. But fear is sometimes just water breaking on the shore."

"I can't just ignore it. It's too painful. I'd rather feel nothing."

Heavenly Bogo looked around at the invertebrates. "These disc anemones are beautiful, right? Simple too. They have no separation between the mouth and anus. It's just one all-purpose opening in their bodies. They don't feel pain. They don't experience fear. Or any other emotion. They just react to physical and chemical stimuli. Do you think creatures with mouth-anuses have all the answers, Leonard?"

I stared at one of the disc anemones, realizing that the puckered knob at its center was eating and pooping at the same time.

"Not a care in the world, these guys. No thoughts or desires either. You wanna be like that?"

I shook my head.

"An abundance of fear is like a virus. Viruses are devoid of reason. They seek only to replicate. Your fear will tell you that you must follow it out of oblivion, but fear is the real oblivion. Resign yourself to the ultimate destruction that we call death, and life will be all the sweeter. Death is the natural mirror of life. See your fear for what it is, a component of you. A tool to be used. That's all."

I didn't want to cry, even underwater. "There were roses in bloom when I left home. I kept thinking that I'd be back real soon. But I'll never get back to that beginning, will I?"

"This moment is one in a series of moments," said Heavenly Bogo. "Each inextricable from the one before and after it. Every version of you exists in tandem, living and dying on axes of probability. Turn to your right. Turn to your left. What did you see? What didn't you see? It is not the direction you turn, but the collection of all your turnings which form you. The mean probability of your frequencies. From a vast multitude of possibilities, the coalescence of your being occurs, bringing you to this time and this place. It brings you to this cavern. It brings you to me."

"I have no idea what you're talking about, Heavenly Bogo. But I'm filled with a vile sadness and I'm drunk on its power all the time. I want to make it stop."

The eel's body glowed, and in its scales my futures were reflected.

Eels couldn't smile. They don't have the muscles for it. It just wasn't something eel jaws could do, even magical, telepathic ones. But Heavenly Bogo smiled. I wasn't projecting myself onto an animal. It was a genuine grin. So real and kind.

I started to laugh. I couldn't help myself. And then Heavenly Bogo started to laugh. There was no sound, no telepathic communication, but its head bobbed up and down and I knew it was a laugh. We laughed together.

"Make with me a covenant, Leonard Marcs. Can you trust me?"

Of course. I already did. I always had.

Heavenly Bogo bit me. Pain—sharper and crueler than any blade—filled my body, but soon dissipated into beestings. When the last of it passed, the eel no longer swam in the water, but upon on the surface of my skin. A living tattoo trailing pixelated bubbles and black movement lines of ink that gradually dissolved.

Chapter 8—More Unexpected Encounters for Leonard

I flexed my bicep and the eel slithered into the crook of my arm.

"Is this how Fishmancers carry their familiars around?" I asked.

Heavenly Bogo chuckled, one of its eyes goggling at me. "I'm not a familiar. I'm the Ninth Lathe of Heaven, called Facilitator. Now listen. We need to get out of the Garden before it's too late. And the only way to do that is through Ml'gyr."

"Did you say Mull-Gear?"

"Yes. Ml'gyr rules this place. They are a being of low cunning and malevolent intentions who has held me captive for many years. The warlocks—the ones you call Fishmancers—serve at their pleasure"

"If Ml'gyr is powerful enough to do that, they'll definitely kill me."

"Nonsense. I am called the Facilitator because I facilitate thy will. I can't facilitate my own—that would be cheating—but now that we're together, we can do anything."

"We still have to find my friend," I said.

"Your friend?" Heavenly Bogo sounded genuinely perplexed.

"Her name's Araxi. The Fishmancers took her hostage."

Heavenly Bogo performed the eel version of a shrug. "I haven't seen anyone like that around."

"How would you know? You've never met her."

"I know what Fishmancers look like. I know how they smell and how they taste. They try to enslave me and I kill them for it. I can tell you that I haven't seen anyone around who *isn't* a Fishmancer. Not lately."

"Maybe Ml'gyr has her trapped in some other reef."

"Ml'gyr doesn't trap humans. Ml'gyr eats them."

I frowned at the eel tattoo. "That's not what I need to hear right now."

"I'm sorry," said Heavenly Bogo, chastened. "That was supposed to sound reassuring."

"Why would that sound reassuring? Oh, nevermind. How did Ml'gyr trap you anyway?"

"I was tricked." The eel skulked into my armpit. "They told me there was something precious here."

"Like a gold deposit?"

"They told me that someone I loved was here. Or would be here. Ml'gyr betrayed my confidence. To think they had once been my friend. I don't wanna talk about it anymore."

I coaxed the eel back onto my bicep and gave its head a stroke. "You're free now, Heavenly Bogo. Let's go kick Ml'gyr's ass."

Kicking ass was not something I was known for, but there was a new power inside me, an energy racing through my nervous system. Like a panic attack, but less overwhelming. My fingers curled. My eyes twitched. I felt unstoppable.

"One of my siblings is the spear," said Heavenly Bogo. "Another the shield. Another the watch, the bridle, the cage, the mirror, the cup, and the wings. Think of me as the wheel. You are already a formidable mechanism, but now interlinked with my power. As you move, so will I, and together we transcend your mortal stride."

My first attempt to have my will facilitated earned me a few broken fingers. The wall of the cavern did not shatter as expected when I punched it.

"Sorry," said Heavenly Bogo, "as you were doing that, it occurred to me that smashing through the rock might cause a catastrophic fissure, killing many innocent corals and fish."

"Then we'll tunnel out," I said.

I pictured the giant rockworm stabbing me through the face with its disgusting needles. Remembered how it had made me crawl. I put myself back in that desperate moment, but now I was in control.

I was the worm. The rock was my medium.

I bit into the rock, and this time Heavenly Bogo facilitated me.

The power was a live wire at the base of my skull. Electricity arcing between my teeth. I sliced through the reef, soft as butter. It tasted like seafood. The chalky gravel scraped my esophagus at first, but soon passed as smooth as cream. My insides were on fire. It was effortless to be the worm, to chew the reef, tunneling blind, yet intuiting which way was up.

I soared in a dream.

By the time I finished eating my way out, I was shedding keratin. Spikes of calcium carbonite erupted from my scalp.

We emerged in a desolate corner of the aquarium where the lights were dim, the water stagnant and rotten. Brown algae covered the glass. No corals or fish to brighten our day.

Ml'gyr appeared from out of the aquarium's deepest wastes. A behemoth scotoplane—a sea pig—striding on gelatinous legs. They fed with a bouquet of suckered tubes that descended two at a time, plucking detritus with metronomic efficiency out of the sand, and shoving the waste into their leering white orifice. A host of shrimps skirted Ml'gyr's undercarriage, mobbing the clouds of silt they dislodged while parasitic gastropods clung to their flanks and burrowed mindlessly into the vast tumescence of their ghostly flesh.

"Now listen," said Heavenly Bogo, curled deep into my ear. "Some crazy shit is about to go down, but I want you to know that no matter what happens, this will all make sense later on."

Ml'gyr encroached upon us, a storm cloud of tentacles, and spoke in a great and terrible voice that rattled me from the brainpan down to my toes.

Another convergence is at hand, Heavenly Bogo, Ninth Child of Leviathan, the Facilitator. Another life to be culled. This occurrence will be the one hundred and twelve thousandth, three hundred and fifty-eighth. And once again, I remain baffled. Why do you insist upon this devastation, O Heavenly Facilitator? This loss perpetual. As always, I offer you the chance to join us and put an end to this conflict.

"The conflict will end," said Heavenly Bogo, "when I have what I want."

Your perseverance resembles madness.

"We only conquer pain by moving through it."

"What are they talking about, Heavenly Bogo?" I couldn't tell if Ml'gyr was able to hear me. "Hey, what're you talking about, you crazy sea pig?"

Ever the fool, this human.

"But he's my fool," said Heavenly Bogo.

Is the Other not also your human?

"The right one collects. The wrong one consumes."

You have a curious mind, Heavenly Bogo.

"I've made my choice. Now give me my pain."

At Heavenly Bogo's insistence, Ml'gyr relinquished a mass of something onto the rocks, and then returned to the wastes without another word.

Ml'gyr's deposit looked a great deal like a turd. Or an egg.

The deposit began to squirm.

A fist punched its way out of the mass, gradually breaking the chitinous enclosure apart. From the pieces, dozens of arms and thousands of teeth emerged. Hands outstretched, mouths open, gullet widening in anticipation.

The face, however, was all too familiar.

My face.

In those pupils, I saw my idiot reflection, struck dumb with terror, unable to stop the image streaking towards the mirror's edge.

A monster reaching through glass to strangle its reciprocal.

I touched the live wire to the base of my skull again.

"Yes, Leonard," said Heavenly Bogo. "That's me. That's our power. Use it."

I swung.

My mirror image was solid steel, collapsing my fist into the arm and shoulder behind it. He hurled me into the reef.

"You're gonna have to try harder than that, buddy," taunted the mirror image in a voice that I had not heard since I was a teenager.

I picked myself up out of the rubble, scarcely believing it.

My face remained on the monster's body, but it swiveled away, crowded out by a new face.

The face of my father, Lionel Anthony Marcs.

"Hey, pal," said my father's face. "How're you doing?"

"Not well, dad." I wanted to lie down. "Not well at all."

"Well, it's gonna get a lot worse before it gets better."

"What, uh, what the fuck are you doing here?"

The monstrous amalgamation put his hands on his hips. "My job."

"Your job, huh?" I looked for Heavenly Bogo but could not find the eel on my arm. "Didn't you die?"

"Think back on it, son. Think real hard. It's not your strong suit, I know, but you'll start to remember if your little friend helps you concentrate."

I closed my eyes and facilitated my own memory. "We buried an arm. That's all we got back. But they told us. They told us you'd died."

"They lied." The amalgamation stretched leisurely. "I was on walkabout. Losing an arm was a real kick in the nads, though. Totally killed my guns akimbo fighting style. But as you can see, I got me a new style, and it's working pretty well."

"And…how exactly did all this come about?"

"Oh, buddy." My father's face chuckled. "I've seen some crazy shit on the Levels. I've seen copies of myself. I've fought myself, won, and eaten the corpse. Many times. It's given me strength. It's how I grew my arm back. But the most shocking encounter was when I found out my old bosses hired my son to be an adventurer. *My* son. I couldn't believe it. And when your boss—ex-boss, I should say—told me what you'd done to get on his shit list, and that you were running amok on the Levels, I figured, hell, maybe there's a little more of me in you than I realized. The reality, unfortunately, is somewhat more disappointing."

"Reality of what, dad?'

"Now, now." The amalgamation advanced. "There's really no point in jawing away. I've done this thousands of times and I'll do it thousands more before this is over."

He reached for me and I snapped off one of his fingers.

"Yowch! Goddammit."

I threw the finger at him. "Why are you doing this?"

"Because they pay me to do it. I'm on the Guild's blacklist, son. A man has to make a living somehow."

We twisted into angry shapes and exchanged blows like dull tremors. Power burned the back of my skull, like fire, reassembled my muscles and knitted my bones, and muted the pain as I was rent and beaten and thrown.

He pinned me to the ground with a fist like an iron spike and shoved a gun in my mouth.

"That which facilitates thy will," read the logogram on its lustrous barrel.

Heavenly Bogo wrapped around my forearm, scales raised in black nettles, a multitude of bloody garnets for eyes, spines trailing long and deadly like jellyfish tentacles. What pity. What sorrow in those eyes. And what anger.

"You lost again, creature," said my father's face. "Better luck next time."

"When you open all the doors, you open every path," replied Heavenly Bogo. "And there is always a path that leads to your end."

He pulled the hammer and the cylinder clicked over.

The shot obliterated me.

For a while, I slept peacefully at the bottom of the ocean.

But when enough of my brain grew back that I could again appreciate the deep pains that were made in my body, I remembered the anti-magic pistol, still tucked into my coat.

My father, crouched above me, smiled triumphantly. "You're meat now. My meat. And your secrets will be mine."

He didn't try to stop me when I fumbled for the bubblegum special.

"The fuck you gonna do with that?" he said. "I'm not made of magic."

"No," said Heavenly Bogo. "But this place is."

I unloaded in all directions. The shots passed through my father harmlessly, but they boiled the ocean in their wake.

I thought I heard Longinus scream.

Chapter 9—Understanding is Not Required

I spat up water, lungs starved for air. Skin covered in sand and broken glass.

Old fluorescent bulbs hummed.

We were back in the store. A massive, shattered aquarium spilled its contents over the floor. Water pumps roared, motors burning out as they sucked in air. Ugly little denizens crawled and flopped about, searching for whatever pools could accommodate them. A tiny diver and a toy statue ran for cover.

I didn't have a chance to stand up.

I was kicked in the head, then the kidney, then the head again.

The amalgamation with my father's face sprawled onto my chest, breathing heavily as his hands closed around my throat. But he didn't squeeze. It seemed like he was waiting for something to happen.

"I subverted you," he panted. "You should be melting."

The more I looked at him, the less I recognized his face.

I smashed his nose with my fist. Energy burning up and down my spine, I picked him up in a ball of flailing limbs and threw him into a bank of aquariums. Glass shards and silver bodies glittered in the rush of floodwaters that turned red with our blood.

He stood again, marred by lacerations, teeth like broken clam shells. "My gun should have turned you into meat. You shouldn't be this hard to kill."

He hit me so hard that my body left a crater. He put hands and claws and feet upon me, dragged me through the shop, and broke dozens of aquariums with my body until we waded in angry fish.

But with each blow, he lost more of his skin. His arms hung loose at his sides. He could barely get up the strength to knock me across the room. Soon, I was lowering him gently to the floor. And where our bodies touched, more of him disappeared.

"How is this possible?" His breath ragged. "My gun was supposed to subvert you. You've subverted me instead. How?"

He ceased struggling and just laid still in my arms.

"Oh, dad." I stroked his cheek. "Didn't you love us? You broke mom's heart."

He chuckled brokenly. "What do you expect me to say?"

"The truth."

"Truth," he scoffed. "I cared for you, didn't I? I wiped your ass. I dried your tears. I put food on the table. By the time I left, Amanda and I were going on five years without so much as a handshake. And you, well, you turned out to be a gigantic pussy. I couldn't be what the two of you wanted me to be. Leaving was the only reasonable thing to do."

"Just like that, huh?"

"Just like that, kiddo." He looked away "A man can only do so much."

"Where did you get this gun?" I picked up his revolver. "You've modified it. This used to be mine."

"Who do you think I got it from?" he said. "Same gun. Different ammunition."

I ejected the last cartridge, held it between two fingers. "It's so heavy."

Blood erupted from his skin like air bubbles from melting ice. "Tritium core. Hyper-dense graviton casing. Plutonium primer—both propellent and Ætheric trigger. The bullet subverts everything it touches, allowing for paradigmatic manipulation in realspace."

"Who would make such a thing?"

"A gift from your old boss." My father coughed up blood. "He told me there were many of you on the Levels. And there are. Doing this, it seemed cruel at first, but you…were so weak. So unprepared. I had to hope this would make you stronger somehow. And it did. Look at you now, Leonard. My boy."

"Do not take credit for this." I glared. "I'm nothing. We're both pawns in this game. I hope the money was worth it."

"That, and so much more." He smiled. "If you're smart, you'll get out of this any way you can. And if you can't, at least have a good time doing it. Pleasure is life's only reward."

"I don't accept that, dad."

"I can't help you make sense of it, buddy. Maybe, when you have children of your own, you'll understand."

"I don't accept that answer." I glanced at Heavenly Bogo, still black with rage. "But, then again, no answer would be sufficient. Therefore, I relinquish you."

"You what?"

"Goodbye, dad. I must talk to myself now."

"What're you doing, Leonard?"

I tore his face off my head and confronted the me that was not me.

The face was mine in every way. But it was older. Angrier.

"The Everybody Company has pitted us against each other," I said. "It doesn't have to be this way."

"Of course it does," my doppelganger replied. "It's the only way."

I leaned in, the two of us cheek-to-cheek. "That's crazy talk. We're on the same side, aren't we?"

He laughed bitterly. "This won't end until every simulacrum is gone. The winner gets to go home."

"I must be pretty fucking stupid. Do you not see how this benefits El Savel? How much stronger we could be if we worked together?"

Our bodies melded. I could feel his thoughts in my head: anger, sadness, mistakes compounding until there was only a single, driving need to consume every version of us that entered the reef.

It wasn't his fault.

Ml'gyr, El Savel, my father—they had used him from the beginning.

"Please answer our father's question," he whispered. "Before I go. How did you resist the bullet? Why did it backfire?"

"It didn't," said Heavenly Bogo. "The bullet worked as intended. The door was open, and two of you walked backwards through it. But this Leonard was stronger, and instead of destroying his frequency, the two of you were joined at the threshold. As it should be."

"I don't really know what that means," said the me who wasn't me.

I shushed him. "Don't worry, neither do I."

I stroked his hair until the last of him disappeared.

Chapter 10—Our Good Times

It was still light out when I left the store.

Great, stabbing pains of hunger chased me all the way to the Worst Friends Hash House where I ordered a Combat Zone with a side of gravy. I'd never eaten anything so wonderful in my life, and was sick for an hour following.

Heavenly Bogo didn't say a word the whole time.

I finally broke the silence. "One hundred and twelve thousand, three hundred and fifty-seven. That's how many copies of me have been absorbed. And I was next. That means one hundred and twelve thousand, three hundred and fifty-eight tritium bullets. That's a lot of expensive, hyper-dense ammunition. Which means either the Company can move through the Levels without being detected, or the Pan Dimensional Services Commission is somehow in on it."

"You wanna do something?" asked Heavenly Bogo suddenly.

"What? This doesn't count?"

"I meant something fun. I've been trapped in an aquarium watching you get eaten by an evil doppelganger for centuries. I need a change of pace."

"What about Anita? What about Level 13? What about defeating El Savel and restoring balance to the Levels?"

"There's time enough." Heavenly Bogo sounded on the verge of tears. "I'm just so happy to see you. I think we should have some fun."

I stroked the eel's head. "Let's get the gang together and watch a movie."

"I would very much like to see them," Heavenly Bogo agreed.

—

"You might say we're tourists," said Punk One.

"You might say we're spectators," said Punk Two.

"We're from a dimension that we affectionally call The Best of All Possible Worlds," said Punk One. "Because that's what it is. The pinnacle of pan-human civilization. Whether destiny—or just some fluke—our society achieved total, biological immortality many centuries ago. We don't experience disease or disability. Each of us attains our physical and emotional prime, and there remains."

"And we've brought back every person who's ever died," said Punk Two. "We can't get maimed. We can't be killed. We don't need anything. Our bodies perpetuate until we decide to stop living, which our technicians can reverse at any time. We live a painless, carefree existence of total equality and peace."

"And it's boring as hell," said Punk One. "If you thought being a tiny speck in a vast, uncaring infinitude made life absurd, try being a tiny speck that can outlive the vast, uncaring infinitude."

"We thought breaking the chains of our mortality would lift our minds to a higher state of consciousness," said Punk Two. "Or at least give us time to work on our novels."

"Turns out, no."

"Not at all. Our idiot brains are perfectly and permanently preserved at a normal level of human awareness. And despite living forever, we don't really change or adapt in any meaningful way. This is as good as we get. Nothing more can be expected from us."

"Hence our one and only problem. Rampant, unquenchable boredom."

"So, we travel the Multiverse, and work in movie theaters and convenience stores and intergalactic politics. Our goal is to observe. We seek out interesting things that our civilization can no longer experience. Hunger, disease, strife. The usual horrors."

"Even small things like embarrassment or gas pain can be entertaining. The kind of stuff that once defined our ephemeral existence and made us strive for immortality in the first place."

I waited to see if they were finished. "All I want are some tickets to *Dick Darkness 2*. Can you do that?"

"Yes, of course, Leonard Marcs," said Punk One.

"You remembered my name?"

"I did, and I owe you an apology," he said. "I thought for sure you were gonna get eaten when you went to the aquarium store. It's happened so many times before, I figured it was just one of those inevitable events. Like the Apocalypse. Or the invention of tacos."

"I told you he was different," said Punk Two.

"You don't have to rub it in."

"And where's your hat? I was promised hat-eating."

"What's the hold up?" demanded Shifty Eyes. "You guys better have a bar back there. I don't see any taps."

"We have something called Beer 12," said Punk One, examining a blue can with the universal logogram for "crunk" on the side. "We don't know where it came from or how we got it. It just showed up in the freezer yesterday. That's the other thing: it doesn't freeze. So, whatever's inside, it's not beer."

"Fine, we'll take the whole pallet," said Shifty Eyes, dumping coins onto the counter. "And will someone get Dead Tomas a napkin? He's oozing all over the pinball machine."

Ron sidled up next to me. "Tomorrow, we all go to Level 13."

"Yes," I agreed.

"So… why are we spending our last night in Castaway at the mall?"

"The mall's not so bad. And Heavenly Bogo wanted a distraction. I figured the movies would be best. Anyway, we're getting drinks afterwards."

"The boys and I have some questions *vis-à-vis* your new eel friend."

"Oh, Heavenly Bogo isn't a new friend. We've known each other for hundreds of years, but I forgot our friendship after El Savel used the Sixth Lathe of Heaven, called Replicator, to turn me into many thousands of simulacra and scatter me across the Levels."

"Right," said Ron. "Let's put a pin in that for now. Just promise me the eel isn't some trickster entity abusing your good nature to further its own dark ends."

"This guy?" I flexed my arm. "Look at those cute little teeth. Look at those flared nostrils. And such beautiful coloration. Heavenly Bogo would never do anything nefarious."

"I feel like you're not taking me seriously."

It turned out that *Dick Darkness 3: Swingin' Dicks* was a coming-of-age story with only a tenuous connection to the characters and setting of the original. The plot centered around a young cockroach person confronting the anxieties of adolescence while chasing her dream of becoming a cockroach private eye and solving cockroach cold cases. The fight choreography wasn't as good as advertised, but we found the performances refreshing and the cinematography majestic.

We drank every can of Beer 12 in the house and started a brawl.

Heavenly Bogo was the sweetest creature that ever lived, but I could feel its desire to kill once the knuckles started flying—wanting to protect me. I kept my head low and assured Heavenly Bogo that everything would be okay.

Then someone pulled an eviscerator and Shifty Eyes lost his temper.

Love was patient and love was kind. Where the lover was concerned.

For everyone else, love was an alligator. Love swam in the same waters as hatred and sorrow. It was cunning and sharp and quick. Love was violent because it came from the heart. Love peeked at you with glowing eyes and drifted closer in the bitter shallows where you dared to linger.

Love knew what you'd done.

Love would catch you and would make you pay.

Love was gonna fuck you up any way it could.

Chapter 11—The Last Days of Castaway

A splitting headache woke me up just before the lasers hit our duplex. The first blast vaporized half the living room where I'd lain moments before, staring at the ceiling. The second blast took the coffee pot right out of my hand.

Ron yelled at me through the wall. "Leonard, what the hell are you doing over there?"

My fingers were badly singed, reluctant to heal up. "We're under attack."

"Having a snack?"

"Under. Attack."

A third blast hit. This time on Ron's side of the house.

"Oh shit, we're under attack! Are you alive? Lenny, speak to me!"

We convened outside. The Fishmancers had stolen my briefcase full of money, and the bubblegum special was toast, but I still had an emergency wad of Guild scrip (redeemable at over five-hundred locations across the Levels). Ron was dressed in full crimson battle regalia and had five swords strapped to his back, with a sixth in hand. It was the sword Howie gave him.

The entire town was being lasered by cyclopean frogmen that towered over the duplexes and office parks, which they crushed beneath amphibian man-feet on their march toward the Guild mansion, blasting psychotronic rays and ululating hymns to the Dark Gods.

Muni cyborgs ran sorties overhead, spraying the frogmen with rockets and bullets and dynamite-covered spears. Casualties were inflicted, but the frogmen were more numerous, and one by one, they blasted our brave Muni boys from the sky. Smaller frogmen waited on the ground and hacked the survivors to bits.

Gore ran thick in the streets.

"We're due at the Elevator in fifteen minutes," I said.

We didn't make it far. A horde of human-sized frogmen blocked the road, waving vorpal axes and swinging chains topped with diamond-studded skulls.

They charged without hesitation.

Ron was a dynamo. A real professional. He killed them like it was going out of style. His love-powered sword wasn't fully activated, but its blade was still made from the same manifold carbons as his armor, and soon it shown with a crimson hue, slicing effortlessly through flesh and bone. But as the bodies piled around him, his movements grew more restricted. The frogmen fell on him en masse.

One frogman slogged away from the orgy of violence and made a beeline for me. I tripped backwards over a corpse. The frogman's jiggling, fish-white belly eclipsed my vision. I raised a hand, and an axe came hissing toward me.

When I blinked, my hand was gone. There was no pressure or pain. I thought of all the delicate little bones and was glad that I wouldn't have to feel them getting trampled.

"I am the Ninth Lathe of Heaven," said Heavenly Bogo in my ear. "Use me. Unleash me. Make thy will manifest. I am Facilitator."

"That was my fucking hand," I told the frogman.

The creature chuckled and raised his axe for another chop.

Eels erupted from my stump. A host of writhing, serpentine bodies in kidney stone colors. They punctured the frogman's abdomen, snaked through his chest, and gorged on his limbs. I felt the eels burrow through his warm innards. In their consumption, I became connected to the frogman too. I heard his thoughts. The creature's fear and confusion. I experienced the agony of being devoured alive by magic eels.

"I'm sorry I lost my temper," I told the frogman. "But you were gonna kill me. I had to do something."

"You are a true agent of death," he said. "An honorable demise. I will be stronger when I am resurrected."

"Who sent you? Was it the Old Ones? The Shrike King?"

"Nah, we're just temps."

"Tell me the name of the staffing agency and I'll eat you fast."

"I can't remember. We use, like, a dozen places. I got a referral through my cousin. Oh God, it hurts so bad. Please let me die."

"Just tell me if it was a place called the Everybody Company. That's all I want to know."

"Hmm. Oh, yeah, that sounds familiar. Everybody Co."

"Are you sure?"

"Positive."

"You're not just telling me what I want to hear?"

His voice gurgled with blood. "Whoever it was, they'll be here soon."

The frogman disappeared into my bouquet of eels.

My hand spontaneously grew back.

The streets piled high with bodies. Half-congealed rivers of blood flowed around my ankles. Shifty Eyes Frank ran in from out of nowhere and punched a frogman in the face so hard its whole head exploded in a shower of green vitae. He grabbed one by the throat and pulled out its tongue. He deflected their axes—the blades crackling against his super-charged skin—and shattered their torsos. He kicked them in half. He tore out their arms and strangled them with their own guts. Together with Ron, their every strike was devastation.

One of the cyclopean giants stomped onto our street, its eye locked on Ron's love-powered sword now covered in amphibian-humanoid guts. It prepared a psychotronic blast that would strip the flesh from our bones.

"That which is dead shall not drink the Vigours of Life," shouted Dead Tomas from the rooftop of a medieval brewpub, "for they are anathema to thee, and will pour from thy mouth untasted, like rain from the gutter."

The giant frogman turned its head and unleashed its pent-up energy on Dead Tomas, annihilating the brewpub, save for its superplastic frame. Dead Tomas remained perched on the skeletal ridge beam, unharmed, but now significantly swollen with the frog's psychic power, a hideous smirk upon his face.

"But where the Vigours of Life are vented in excess, even the Valley of Death may yet bear fruit." His corpulent torso writhed. "Life will make a bed in any soil, for that is the way and the will of Life. And verily, it was."

Dead Tomas pulled his bloated belly apart, and from its oily depths, a fiendish mass clawed forth. A howling maw of teeth with vestigial eyes, its sleek and chitinous frame hissed with smoke as Castaway's thrice-purified atmosphere burned in its lungs.

The demon vaulted from Dead Tomas' ruptured stomach and went straight for the frogman's psynetic eye, popping it like a grape. The frogman tried desperately to pry the demon out, but soon collapsed in the street where the demon burrowed into the amphibian's braincase and there expired, writhing and spitting acid that melted the frogman's head down to the vertebrae.

Warships descended from the Mezzanine and their silvery hulls gleamed in the late afternoon sun. Laser lights flickered and ion cannons zapped. Flocks of smaller assault craft fanned out from their carriers in perfect formation and went after the remaining giants

"I think the Municipal Navy can take it from here," said Ron, his moustache dripping with entrails.

Shifty Eyes wasn't having it, still hyped up on rage juice and punching frogmen into goop.

Dead Tomas made it down from the roof and staggered over, his bowels hanging from his torso like party streamers. "Phew. Glad that little dickens is finally out of my body cavity."

I gave him and Ron a hug. "The frogs were just cannon fodder. The people who hired them are coming next, and they'll be a lot tougher."

"How do you know this?" asked Ron.

"No time to explain," I said. "We can't be late."

We found Shifty Eyes wandering amidst a pile of corpses two blocks away, still deep in his beserk state, but amenable to following us when we told him we knew where to find more things to kill.

We recognized many of the dead as we ran to the Elevator.

We turned a corner, and where there should have been a block of apartments, there was now a large pyramid on a steaming bed of wreckage. The pyramid's edifice was a network of gleaming geodesics, the composition irregular and mafic. A light emanated from its base, turning the crushed buildings underneath into neon gravel. It hummed softly.

"They're already here," I said.

"Who's here, Lenny?" asked Dead Tomas, eternally optimistic.

I turned to them. "I have to tell you something very important."

The pyramid's surface shifted suddenly and a great, baleful eye emerged, its iris the color of steel, its pupil wide and shining. The eye leered at us for a second, then turned skyward and emitted a beam of light. Clouds fled at its approach. The beam pierced a Municipal frigate, erupted undiminished out the frigate's stern, and exploded against the sky-ceiling.

There came a loud groaning of metal as the frigate's integrity was compromised. It sank gently, pulsing with klaxons, before a second and third beam struck, detonating the ship's power core. In quick succession, laser beams skewered the entire Muni fleet. Warship *hors d'oeuvres.*

A cascade of nuclear meltdowns followed.

The ground undulated with shockwaves and the sky filled with towers of white-hot clouds. After the heat flayed me to the bone and a cocoon of blinding energy carried me off to dreamland, I realized what had happened.

My eyes grew back after a long silence.

Rubble buried me. Hair and flesh were gone. My body regenerated itself, but slowly. Pain morphed gradually from agony to itchiness.

I looked for my friends when I could move again.

They were underneath me. Little more than skeletons wrapped in ash.

A handful of Muni ships remained airborne, wreathed in flames.

Their lifeless hulks drifted into a scorched horizon.

Chapter 12—Back in Bastion City, When Life Made Sense

"Why the hell would I buy a coupon?" demanded the potential investor. "People just give those things away."

"You don't understand, sir. Coupon is a financial term that refers to the annual interest rate paid on a debt obligation. The Municipal Traders Coupon Book is a portfolio of corporate bonds, each with coupons that can be separated."

"Yeah? So why does this one say 25% off your entire meal? That sounds like a regular damn coupon to me."

"These corporate bonds are also a special type of convertible bond," I explained. "Rather than wait for the bonds to mature, you can convert them to discounts on goods and services. This Big Ed's Hotcake note, for example, has a face value of fifty dollars, and will mature in two years. But if you were to spend five hundred dollars at Big Ed's, converting the bond to a 25% discount would represent a substantial windfall."

The potential investor squinted at the fine print. "Who the hell is going to spend that much on pancakes?"

"You might not, but maybe you know someone who will. You can buy this bond from me at a ten percent discount, strip the coupons, and then trade it to a birthday party or a breakfast club. Anything's possible."

"So how come you're selling it?"

"Trust me," I said, affecting a brotherly tone, "I'd love to just wait around and get my principal back, but I need the scratch."

"That so?" The potential investor loomed. "I'll take it for half off."

"Be reasonable. This isn't a yard sale."

"You said you needed the money. Deal or no deal."

I paused for effect. "I'll tell you what. You can have the Big Ed's note and these Waffle Bivouac bonds together for seventy cents on the dollar."

The potential investor did the math. "Done. Hand them over."

"May the Universal Spirit bless you and keep you. Now, if I can just scan your retina…"

"I don't have a retinal hookup. Cash only."

"Even better, sir. Even better."

The certificates were printed with inks that could be tracked by any headhunter worth their salt. His signature was immediately sent to the Investment Commission, with copies registered on both the Bastion City Commerce Blockchain and Frick's personal server. We each signed a paper receipt and swapped carbon copies. As soon as the money changed hands, the new investor booked it down an alley as if fleeing a crime, which it technically was.

What I never told our investors was that debt obligations issued by corporations not headquartered in Bastion City—even when those obligations were issued in Bastion City dollars—were subject to punishingly-high capital gains taxes in an effort to promote local investment. Legally, we could assume that any savvy investor would know this, or so Frick liked to argue. Frick, of course, acquired the Municipal Trader's Coupon Book for practically nothing.

It was finally payday, and not a moment too soon.

Frick transferred my paycheck and bid me a good weekend.

I returned to the Order of the Sublime Reliquary Flophouse, scenically buried beneath ten blocks of warehouses and server farms. There were a few loft apartments, but most of the neighborhood lived in capsule hotels just like mine.

A hallway party was already in full swing. We had two hundred people on our floor, each of them with friends and lovers to contribute. There was booze. There were pills. There were strange root vegetables consumed by eager-eyed denizens in full-length robes. The place was a rager.

I ran into El Savel sooner than I thought. He was deep in the throes of something fun, his hands crawling like spiders over an attractive humanoid who had moved in last week. The two of them danced off-tempo to the hallway music.

His eyes were the size of dinner plates when he saw me. "Lenny, my man! I was just thinking about you."

"Probably because my rent is due in less than five minutes," I said.

"You're a good tenant. And a good friend. Have I ever told you that?"

I tried to not roll my eyes. "Can we step into your office?"

The attractive humanoid gave El Savel a deep kiss and sashayed away, swallowed up in the chaos of the party.

"Easy come, easy go," he said with a shrug, swaying in place.

I could hear the security orcs nearby. It didn't matter if El Savel was too fucked up to register my rent. They would start the eviction process the instant the clock hit zero. I dragged my landlord into his suite and got the process going. I was paying in some new cryptocash that earned me a 10% discount.

"You ever been to the Portals, Lenny? It's an amazing sight." El Savel stared at the ceiling. "People think the city was built inside of a box for its own protection, and that's also true I guess, but the real reason—"

"Shit, it's not working," I said.

"Whaddya mean it's not working?"

"The transaction won't go through. It says your identity can't be verified."

"Yours? Or mine?"

"Your wallet's identity."

"That's ridiculous." El Savel snatched the phone out of my hand. "The wallet is just an address. It either exists or it doesn't. Ah, here's the problem. You're using Lemon Pay. Why are you using Lemon Pay?"

"They said it was a good app."

"Well, it's not. Use anything but Lemon Pay. Hold on, I know a workaround. Look at you. You're like a baby sea gull paddling over a school of sharks."

"Have you ever been to an ocean, El?"

"Now, listen, because we need to talk about something important. The reason they built Bastion City the way they did."

"I'm not a dropout," I said, not in the mood for one of his rants. "I know all about Ley Lines and Star Titans and the Prime Gnosis. Yadda yadda yadda."

"You most certainly do not. The Order of the Sublime Reliquary—"

"Oh here we go."

"Do not interrupt your landlord!"

I sighed with relief as my rent payment finally processed. "You already know I'm not interested in your religion. Or any religion."

"This isn't religion, bro." He scowled and poked my chest. "I'm talking about the future, Lenny. The Order of the Sublime Reliquary has plans. You've been following the latest Hero War?"

"Who hasn't. It's all over the feeds. You can't get away from it."

"The Castaways don't stand a chance. And when it's over, who do you think is positioned to control the Levels?"

"The Coalition, I assume."

"Yeah, but what members of the Coalition? The first one down the Elevator, that's who."

"What's your point?" I asked, yearning to check out the party.

"It's the Portals, stupid—the reason Bastion City was built in a box. We've got portals to every Ley Line Node in the Multiverse. We're the ultimate city state because we're the ultimate trading partner. And once the embargos are lifted, one of the most important Nodes in existence will be on our shortlist. Direct access to Level 1."

An eerie calm washed over us. I couldn't gauge his mood, but I'd never seen El Savel look so serious, especially not when high off his ass.

"You think I don't know why you're in Bastion City?" he said, grinning and stooping low. "I know all about you. Your dreams. Your ambitions. That token you carry everywhere—your father's tattoo."

I almost reached for the pendant. "That's none of your business."

"It's the whole reason you came here."

"I came here for a lot of things."

"I looked him up, your father. A classic adventurer. Plundering, whoring, swashbuckling. Died young doing what he loved. Real old school. I respect that. Would have liked to meet him. But you're lucky he's been dead awhile, or Immigration might have hauled you off with the other Castaways."

I tried to edge for the door but El Savel took me by the shoulders. He was surprisingly strong. His breath smelled like a root vegetable.

"You're not cut from the same cloth as your old man—that much I can tell—but you want to be an adventurer just like him. You want to finish his quest. The quest he died for. You know who gave him that quest?"

I pulled myself free. "He gave it to himself. He had to stop a terrible evil from collecting the Lathes of Heaven and conquering the Multiverse."

El Savel shook his head. "The Order of the Sublime Reliquary commissioned him. We were the ones who taught him all about the Lathes and their importance. Don't believe me? We've got facsimiles of his W-2, his weapons license, his life insurance policy, everything. This was long before I joined the Order, but it's all in the archives, perfectly and permanently preserved."

I wanted this rant to be joke, but I couldn't fathom how it was supposed to be funny. "Why didn't you tell me this before?"

"Because I needed to know you weren't just a giant flake. I mean, let's be honest, I had my concerns. You didn't pay your rent on time, you didn't keep regular hours, and you didn't show up for any of the floor meetings."

"There were floor meetings?"

"I was afraid you were just another weekend warrior. One more body for the slag heap of this beautiful, wretched city. But you turned it around, Lenny m'boy, and I'm proud of you."

It seemed so absurd, but the more I thought about it, the less skeptical I became. The Order was one of countless, overstuffed cliques affecting a nobler image, yet its milieu had a way of attracting actual adventurers. People I'd heard of too, like the Mighty Minotaur, who would occasionally visit The Lounge. Though brief, these encounters were never inconsequential. Combined with the Order's non-descript esotericism and apparent foothold in the dirt-cheap housing market, it was exactly the sort of organization my old man would have fallen in with, and just the sort of organization to get him his start in the business.

"On behalf of the Order of the Sublime Reliquary, I'd like to offer you a job as a fulltime adventurer," said El Savel. "Comes with a lot of perks. No more rent. Free access to any of our fine facilities across the Multiverse. Health clubs, night clubs, bars, temples, you name it. Flophouses are just the tip of the iceberg."

"This is all a bit overwhelming," I said. "I need time to think."

"More like time to *drink*. But seriously, don't think too hard. This is your dream, Leonard."

"What about this new guild the Coalition is proposing? After they reconquer the Levels, every adventurer will have to sign up."

"That's why you can't afford to waste time! The Order will advocate for its people—get them grandfathered in or out of whatever bullshit regulations they impose. And keep in mind, finding the Lathes of Heaven is our quest. That's proprietary. You can't get that from another agency. But maybe I'm rushing things. I've dropped a bombshell on you. Take the night off. What you need to do is press the flesh. Get out there and meet some folks."

We rejoined the party. El Savel was charming when he wanted to be. It didn't take long for me to start feeling bad about giving him lip. I was his best friend within an hour. I was everyone's best friend within two.

Of course I'd be honored to work for the Order of the Sublime Reliquary!

There was no reason to even hesitate.

I met so many faces. So many names that I would never remember.

Not that any of them would remember mine. That's how parties were supposed to work. No more niceties. No more decorum. Just do what you feel. A reprieve from reality.

I was a river of booze unto my liver.

I attracted the gaze of a woman. Human, like me.

"You remember me?" she asked.

"How could I forget," I said.

A woman with eyes like two primary moons, and a gorgeous, guttural laugh. She stood close to me throughout the evening, even when I was loud. A woman with fire on her breath. A woman with hair that sparkled like volcanic glass, that felt like silk between my fingers.

I asked if she would remind me of this night—and of her—when I had forgotten everything. Because I knew that I would. Forgetting things was what I did. Especially when drunk.

She said yes. And I forgot that too.

—

I got a gig cleaning offices on the upper levels of Centercrown Arcology, simultaneously high above the city lights and closer than ever to the antipode of glowing, crystalline spires that substituted the night sky. On the floors above were penthouses of mythic opulence, always thrumming with music, their elevators heavily-guarded by flawless killing machines, which would occasionally follow us around as we worked.

My new position with the Order of the Sublime Reliquary would remain an abstract concept until the Hero Wars ended. And since I already quit working for Frick, I was stuck temping.

It wasn't so bad. Maximum flexibility with minimum responsibility. A decent wage too, if you didn't mind living in a capsule the rest of your life. The hook, line, and sinker of Bastion City.

Just about everyone worked for a temp agency at one point in their careers, but the barrier separating the gainfully employed from a vast, part-time underclass was only eight months, a year at most if the agency was reputable. That's how long a person could temp. After that, if you didn't have a real job, you were marked as a perma-temp. Tantamount to a bum.

Working in Frick's living room didn't exactly count as a real job, even with fulltime hours. And though I was technically employed by the Order, any landlord could look at my bank account and connect the dots. The only thing worse than having no job was having a job that didn't pay. It showed a lack of initiative, they said. Made people think, "Hey, this guy is happy to earn nothing. That's not the kind of energy we need."

A few nights later, it turned out someone on our crew stole office supplies, so they fired all of us for good measure.

I eventually got a new gig processing sausage at a vertical meatfarm.

On day five, my hair and clothes stinking of cultured flesh, I returned home to find Anita waiting outside my capsule. She had a smile on her face, her arms crossed, head back against the wall. She looked good in a tight blue jumper.

"Good morning, Leonard," she said.

"Anita." A sudden pain erupted in my head.

"You work too much," she said, still smiling. "I've been by your place three times this week. You should take a vacation."

"Wish I could afford it," I said, guts squirming.

"Really? Not even for a night? Not even to go to a party?"

Memories vomited up into my brain, and I might have run from her out of sheer mortification if I had anywhere to go. "It was you. That night."

"Uh huh." She pulled her arms behind her back, stretching the jumper's fabric even tighter.

"I never called."

"Didn't have to call." She swayed. "We're neighbors. You could've just left a note. I would've given you a key."

I almost choked.

"But," she said, "you warned me fair and square. You're a forgetter."

"It's been a problem all my life. Feels like I'm too stupid to be alive sometimes."

"There's no need for self-deprecation." Her smile never faltered. "You also told me to remind you. It was 'the best night of your life,' you said."

"Oh god."

"It was very endearing. So here I am, dropping in like a good neighbor to say," she paused, and walked over to put her hands on my shoulders, "hello, Leonard Marcs, please don't forget about the best night of your life. And maybe take a girl out for a drink sometime. But not too many drinks."

I put my hands on her hips and she floated into me.

"Less of my brain gets in the way when I'm drunk," I said as she tucked her head under my chin.

"You were certainly very direct."

"I didn't forget you. Not in the bad way."

She laughed. "There's a good way to forget someone?"

"It's hard to explain…my brain is like an alligator."

"Beg pardon?"

"Some things—important things—are like alligators in my mind. Dangerous things. The alligators lurk in the rivers of my brain. And my brain says it's easier to forget than to be frightened. But an alligator doesn't just go away. It strikes. When the time is right. The alligators remind me of things that are real."

"Am I an alligator?"

"Oh definitely."

"And important, huh?"

I blushed.

"Well, the alligator is here." She clacked her teeth. "What happens now?"

"Well, you might not mind it," I said with a chuckle, "but I need a shower. I just pulled a ten-hour shift at Autentico Salami."

She breathed deep. "You smell like a sandwich."

"And you smell…amazing. What's that perfume?"

"I don't wear perfume," she whispered. "That's just me."

—

El Savel slapped me so hard I felt my teeth loosen.

"I need you in the zone, Lenny. This is war, you understand? Forget everything else except the job at hand. Focus on the now."

He slapped me again.

If I thought about the now, I'd have to ask myself once again why we were hunting down fellow members of the Order. I'd have to consider the repercussions of our betrayal, and contemplate once more the evidence of their wrongdoing. Even if true, the evidence was tenuous all the same.

El Savel's word against theirs.

And if I thought too hard, I'd have to acknowledge the ugly things that nagged me. The blackness that spread in my mind as I tried to rationalize our course of action. And if that came to pass, I might have to run away. Take Anita into hiding and run as far as we could go.

I would have to become an anonymous temp once more.

That, most of all, was something I did not want to contemplate.

My revulsion was an alligator, and I let it swim away.

"Sixty seconds," said El Savel. "Lock and load."

The Portals were in a subterranean vault equal in size to Bastion

City's primary living sphere. The space was solely dedicated to commerce, with hundreds of interstellar and interdimensional exchanges based in this one massive room. The weight of the wealth that changed hands, flippers, claws, and tentacles with each passing moment staggered the mind.

It was a dangerous place in theory because you never knew what evils might try to push their way through the Portals. In practice, the real dangers were already in the room. Being a hub for interdimensional travel, the Portals were not strictly owned by Bastion City. They were jointly guarded by the politically-agnostic forces of the Pan-Dimensional Services Commission with whom Bastion City shared an old and acrimonious relationship.

Our success today hinged on exploiting that acrimony.

Members of the Order emerged from the Level 1 Portal, eight of them carrying a grand palanquin on which the Twin Voices reclined. They had just finished this year's Grand Quest to the Level of the Wonder Khan and the Golden Horde, their caravan now laden with splendid opals, fleeces, scimitars, and jars of rare honey. None of which we desired.

According to El Savel, these men had cleaned out the Order's rarest assets from the Sublime Reliquary and traded them on Level 13 to a young adventurer named Wolfram Selma. What they supposedly received in trade was a mythical treasure plucked from the very hands of Bob Alpha himself.

This treasure—El Savel claimed—was a Lathe of Heaven.

How a mere child had slain Bob Alpha was something else again, but rumors from the field held no evidence to cast doubt on her exploits. The doubt remained with El Savel's report. Surely nothing in all the Reliquary's vaults could match the value of such a prize. Unless Wolfram Selma knew not what she had won.

Our targets crossed the mark.

There was a moment between moments when I thought I might do the opposite of what I did. A moment after the handle had turned but before the door was opened. A moment which held out hope that I would not walk through.

Our crossbows went off in a small clatter and ran our old coworkers through with cyanide-tipped bolts.

The palanquin crashed to the floor. Explosives detonated. The temps we hired began screaming at once, using all manner of slurs and contradictory codewords intended to incite many groups at once.

The Bastion City Police Department and the Pan-Dimensional

Services Commission were soon at each other's throats, tearing portals apart in the crossfire of their deadly instrumentation. Others joined without hesitation, adding their own vendettas and blood feuds to the pall of violence that hid us from scrutiny.

After a few more rounds of crossbow fire, we approached the downed palanquin. The conjoined twins were filled with bolts—enough poison to kill someone ten times their size—but still they fought us, swinging golden knives that burned the air. El Savel fought to snatch the prize around their necks. After a protracted struggle, he demanded a crossbow, and put a bolt in their sternum.

"At least die with some dignity," he spat.

We bolted their arms to the ground and the knives fell from their hands.

The Twin Voices seemed to give up completely, their heads limp, eyes darting furiously around the trading floor. "Many will die for this ambition of yours, El Savel. Can you live with that?"

El Savel shrugged. "They know what they do. If they would rather kill each other, who am I to stand in their way?"

The Twin Voices coughed up blood. They had no strength to resist when El Savel finally removed their pendant. A small and cloudy globe. El Savel studied it for a long moment but was eventually satisfied and pocketed the orb without comment.

"Well?" I asked.

"Well what?" demanded El Savel.

"Is that what we came here for?" I had a sudden need to see the orb. "Was it worth it?"

"More than worth it," said El Savel, patting his pocket and smiling at the Twin Voices. "A treasure beyond all treasures."

The Twin Voices, our former leadership, gave each of us a look that went right to the bone. "We have already used the Lathe's power. We shall return, traitors, and there is nowhere in all the Multiverse you can go that we won't find you. Sanity shall be restored to the Order."

El Savel produced a knife. "That's the trouble with you two. For all your gifts, even your foresight, you lack real vision. The Order means nothing. It never did. But this wondrous item—a Lathe of Heaven—it means everything. In time, our works will define the Multiverse itself."

He sliced their throats.

"The Order of the Sublime Reliquary exists no more," he said to us. "From now on, we represent our own corporation. Long live the Everybody Company."

Chapter 13—The Remnants of Castaway and Our Carefully Laid Plans

The Company pyramids took off into the sky, trailing wreckage and kicking up great clouds of dust. Their engines sent shockwaves through Castaway's ruins, leveling the last standing structures. Whoever might have survived the frogmen and the nuclear firestorm was surely dead by now.

The fleet gathered energy, built to a deadly crescendo, and vanished with a dimensional pop, bound perhaps for another unsuspecting town to demolish.

My friends were gone.

Everyone was gone.

Except Anita, I hoped. But to where? It was not for me to know.

What a ridiculous, self-obsessed piece of shit I was, to have worried so much about myself, to have felt so frightened by all the unfolding complexities. I had never been in danger. It was everyone else I should have worried about.

"It'll be okay," said Heavenly Bogo.

I stared off into the wreckage of my home. "When we met, you said that I was the mean probability of my frequencies. What does that mean?"

"It's like this," said Heavenly Bogo evenly. "Your existence is the result of a great hyperhedron of possibilities that are constantly in flux. Think of it as a cosmic equation that must be balanced by isolating variables. These variables are produced by a functionally-infinite number of parallel realities in which the totality of all your possible choices and experiences occur simultaneously. You can't be everywhere, and probability says you have to be somewhere, so here is where you end up."

"But I was replicated," I said. "I'm not just here. I'm all over the place. What does that do to my equation?"

"Oh, hard to say. Like me—like all our siblings—Heavenly Nyos, the Sixth Lathe of Heaven, called Replicator, functions at a transcendental frequency that predates material existence. But Heavenly Nyos and I comprehend the Multiverse in very different ways. My powers rest within the limitless potential of the individual. The powers of the Replicator rest within the limitless potential of paradigmatic variability. From what I understand of cosmic equations, the Replicator's powers shouldn't even be possible."

"Are you saying you don't understand your own siblings?"

"Each Lathe is master of its own domain. But we were made to balance each other out. There's nothing that one of us can do that another can't undo. I've fought against my own siblings many times."

I thought on this awhile. "Suppose these copies of me aren't copies at all, but different frequencies balanced into existence by the Replicator?"

"As good an explanation as any I guess."

"And if all my frequencies are here, what else did they bring with them? Are there other frequencies of Castaway? Other frequencies of my friends?"

Heavenly Bogo didn't seem to enjoy this line of inquiry. "If there are, I wouldn't suggest you go looking for them."

"Why the hell not?"

Heavenly Bogo fixed me with a round, fishy stare. "You trod the path to insanity, Leonard. I have met many of your frequencies and you have diverged from none of them in any meaningful capacity, save one: a lack of obsession. Please don't start now."

"Do the Lathes of Heaven experience love?"

Heavenly Bogo looked hurt. "Of course."

"Then you know I have to save my friends. That's love, not obsession."

"You're trapped in a terrible cycle, Leonard, and it all starts here. The only way to save yourself is to allow Castaway to be destroyed."

It finally dawned on me. "You've known this whole time what was going to happen."

Heavenly Bogo didn't look away from me. "There was no alternative. I'm trapped in a cycle just as you are. "

"Then we were never friends. You were just using me."

"Leonard, no! I've always been your friend. Since the first day we met. Please believe me. Listen—"

"Oh, good, you're still alive," interrupted a familiar voice.

It was Araxi. And next to her was Rolla, and behind them, a phalanx of guys in identical black armor, armed to the teeth.

They approached us from all sides.

"We were ready to give up," said Rolla, her own black armor poorly fitted to her rotund and soggy form. "The explosions must have damaged your tracker."

They looked expectantly at me, but I was so numb I could hardly respond.

Araxi cleared her throat. "Been a while, Leonard. I was hoping we'd wrap things up with the Fishmancers sooner. Didn't expect you to forget all about me…"

I gestured at the wreckage. "Was this your doing?"

Rolla chuckled. "What kind of question is that? You saw the whole thing. Those pyramids were from the Everybody Company."

Araxi approached, full of consternation. "Are you alright?"

"No, I'm not alright!" I said. "Castaway's gone and everyone's dead. And you were in on it. How could you?"

"Settle down." Rolla's hackles rose. "Yes, we knew the attack was coming. Because there's always an attack. They think they've killed you. We make sure that doesn't happen. Just like last time. And every time before that."

"You tricked me," I said. "You used me to get Heavenly Bogo out of the aquarium store. And then…"

"Yes, and then what?" Araxi's third eye glowed. "We've seen Castaway destroyed thousands of times, Leonard. We've had this conversation thousands of times. Only now have we something to show for it."

The back of my throat felt like sandpaper. "Why couldn't someone just tell me the truth?"

"This is fucking tedious." Rolla marched over and slapped a badge in my hand. "Does that ring any bells?"

It was a Guild license with my picture—the same one I carried around—but the rest of the information was missing. No name. No Designation. Not even vitals or an organ-donor's watermark. It was a blank slate waiting to be filled in.

A fake ID.

"You work for us," said Araxi. "You always have."

I mouthed the words back at her. "But I don't remember—"

"You don't remember because you weren't supposed to remember," said Araxi. "Not until you secured the objective."

"I normally hate absentminded people," said Rolla, "and you're hardly what I would call an exception, but you have an extraordinary ability to compartmentalize sensitive information, which has made you valuable."

"I don't understand," I said.

"Like a broken record," said Rolla with disgust. "Look, when people have a secret, they normally lie about it. You, on the other hand, don't have to lie because you can selectively repress memories that you consider important. No one can force the information out of you because you won't even remember you have it."

"I know this is a lot to process," said Araxi, trying to take my hand. "Just come with us and we'll get you debriefed. I promise, it will all come back to you."

"After you deliver the weapon," interjected Rolla.

I waited for them to say more. "What weapon?"

"This fucking guy," said Rolla. "What weapon. The Lathe of Heaven, you egregious dullard. The whole reason you're here."

"The Nine Lathes are the most powerful weapons in all known reality," said Araxi. "Do you remember? From the stories? Only they're not stories. The Lathes of Heaven are real, and you were sent here to find one."

"He must have repressed the memories too deeply." Rolla tried to clap me on the ears. "Hello! Anyone home in there? It's time to wake up and give your superior officers the Lathe of Heaven so we can finally stop the Company and be done with this insultingly stupid mission."

Heavenly Bogo was plainly visible on my arm for all of them to see, but none of them took any notice. They thought it was just a tattoo.

"You don't know," I whispered. "You don't know what the Lathes of Heaven actually are. You have no idea what you're dealing with."

"Is that so?" Rolla drew a pistol and pointed it at my knee. "You have exactly ten seconds to snap out of whatever fugue is clouding that tiny brain of yours before I snap you out of it myself."

Araxi reached for the gun. "There's no need for this."

"You're on his side now?" Rolla snarled.

"Leonard is our coworker. Our friend."

"He's no friend of mine. He was always a goddamn sneak. A weirdo. He stole from the fridge and took long bathroom breaks. He fell upwards into promotions. I've always hated him."

"Be that as it may, Rolla, my love, I am compelled by my code as a Person Resources Officer to prevent you from shooting a fellow agent."

"I'm not giving you Heavenly Bogo," I said. "Even if I wanted to, I don't think I could."

Rolla's snout twitched. "Are you disobeying a direct order?"

"I don't care who I used to work for," I said. "No reality exists where you get the Ninth Lathe of Heaven."

"Debatable." Rolla shot my leg off at the knee.

"Rolla, goddammit!" shrieked Araxi.

"Relax," said Rolla. "He'll grow a new leg in no time."

I was deep in a pool of my own blood and the stump wasn't healing.

Something was wrong with my nanites. The wound staunched as new skin flowed to cover the mangled injury, but that was all. I scrabbled for my disembodied leg, hoping that it would reattach, but the flesh grew calloused and thick, rejecting the moribund object.

"Don't worry," said Rolla to the guys in identical black armor, "it's nearly impossible to kill him. Shoot off the other limbs if he resists."

"Stop it!" yelled Araxi. "His body isn't regenerating. Something's wrong."

Rolla's face was overtaken with sadistic joy. "The Company must have shut off his medical fog. He blew his cover."

"We need to get him stabilized," said Araxi.

Rolla shouldered past her. "Out of the way, Agent Arshakuni. Your infatuation for this human has caused us enough trouble. He's dog meat once we get him to headquarters."

I should have tried to reason with them, but the sight of their guns—the contempt on Rolla's face—drove all emotion from my body.

"Canst thou draw me out with a hook?" asked Heavenly Bogo to the assembled crowd. "Canst thou open the doors of my face? Lay thine hand upon me, and remember. I laugh at thy spear. I laugh at thy double bridle."

Rolla glanced at the others. "Did that tattoo just talk?"

I didn't need nanites to survive. I was eels. Eels all the way down.

I overflowed. They opened fire without hesitation. I moved around their projectiles, swallowing whole the destruction they tried to bestow and gifting it back. I tore the guns from their hands and hollowed their bodies from bone to skin, leaving nothing but eels in my wake.

I was blind and indiscriminate.

And then, not even their husks remained.

All of them were gone in seconds. Even Araxi, who had only tried to help.

—

My severed leg turned into eels and eventually reattached itself.

Heavenly Bogo and I picked our way across the rubble of Castaway.

Flaming battleships fell to plowshares and the ground danced under my feet. Patches of my skin molted from the radiation. I puked until there was nothing left to squeeze out.

Despite the devastation, the delicate thread of the Elevator remained intact. Its platform was covered in wreckage, but otherwise undamaged.

A group of adventurers had died right outside its doors, their bodies scattered like divining bones.

"I really wish I could dissuade you from this," said Heavenly Bogo.

My hands shook as they hovered over the panel of buttons. "Just tell me which ones to press."

The Elevator started up and Castaway shrank to an ugly smear on the prairie.

My stomach dropped as we picked up speed.

We hit the limits of the skybox and the ambient light source that we called the sun disappeared. This was normally where the Elevator would kick into high gear, but things went silent and still. I no longer felt the Elevator moving.

I no longer felt anything at all.

Conveyed skyward through memories and dreams, we ascended new realms into Levels without numbers. In that lightless place, I saw two versions of myself. One caked in the filth of memories—some repressed, some mundane, added layer upon layer with each passing moment—and the other clean of all context. Like a newborn lamb. The two versions met, and in touching, produced endless numbers of myself that spread in clonal colonies across the Multiverse.

Look down.

Look up.

What did I see?

A child at the beginning. The first moment among moments when I became human. A corpse at the end. The final version when all versions collapsed into one and were gone forever.

I was a serpent and I bit my tail. I could swallow myself whole if I wanted

I was a hydra, with many heads and many tails to bite. I could feed on myself forever. Sprouting, always, new heads and new tails. Within that tangle was my origin and my terminus. The last of me. The first of me.

The mean probability of all my frequencies.

Mechanisms clicked into place and motors engaged.

Lights returned in washed out colors.

The Elevator came to a stop, announcing our Level in a language of broken harmoniums and crooked birds.

The digital display read 159,000,000,000,000,110,896.

The light was perverse somehow. I could see it, but it didn't make sense. It was like staring at a blur. Something intended for alien eyes.

"This is the Celestial Level," said Heavenly Bogo. "The Star Titans built it trillions of times removed from the Cardinal Levels to preserve the integrity of the construct, and to prevent their demi-celestial offspring from using the Levels to harm them. Which is exactly what happened, just not in the way they expected."

I touched the glass of the Elevator door and it turned warm. "This is where you're from?"

"I'm not *from* anywhere. But this is where Leviathan was imprisoned after our defeat, and where the Star Titans dismantled us, severing our collective consciousness into nine entities. We like to think of it as the place we grew up."

Something approached, a blur shifting quietly into form.

"Oh," said Heavenly Bogo, "has one of them come to meet us?"

The shape resolved. Just a man. A man who both was and wasn't me.

He stood within the vapors of the Celestial Level without a care, indifferent to the unreality of this divine place.

He wore the sickest gear.

"I see you checking out my gear," he shouted through the glass. "Come on out and let me tell you about it."

I was drawn to him and stepped from the Elevator without complaint. The air was thick but not unpleasant. Cold and hot at the same time. Exotic shapes briefly coalesced and were swallowed again by the mist.

We stood facing one another like mirrored images. I might have heard Heavenly Bogo talking, but couldn't understand a word the creature said.

"My name is Lionel Anthony Marcs Jr. But you can call me Larry."

"I won't," I said. "That's a terrible name."

"Which part?"

"All of it. I hated our father and I don't like the name Larry."

"I've traveled far and wide across these Levels," said Larry, unfazed. "Seen a lot of things. Killed many enemies. Met my fair share of…replicants. What name do you go by?"

"Leonard. Friends called me Lenny."

"A classic. And what are your accomplishments, Leonard?"

"I was an underemployed binge drinker. Then someone put a fish on my door and thrust me into this convoluted conspiracy against my will."

Larry shook his head. "Every one of us got the Mana Fish. It happened the same way each time. But don't think it wasn't according to plan. It was our plan. We're all fighting the same fight. We always have been. It's just that none of us remembers all the pieces. Lost to the gators, as we say."

"I'm really interested in your gear for some reason," I said in a daze. "You look like you've been out here a long time."

"This ensemble is a labor of love," said Larry, gesturing at his clothes. "The boots are made from ascendant nacrohide, a material that looks and feels like kid leather, but is virtually indestructible. Can't scuff it. The fibers of this trench coat were woven from the tears of a Septagomis Volrak—also indestructible—but capable of transforming into a giant bat. There are only four such coats like this in existence and three of them are navy blue. Mine is black. This beautiful vest is genuine sea silk embroidered with anti-magic pearls made by the last arch-wizard, Gugul Caih Ahn-Ro. The shirt and pants are some nanotech bullshit, but they can imitate any fabric I want, and are basically indestructible as well. Also, the pants turn into shorts with a snap of my fingers."

"It's all very impressive," I said. "I think I need to sit down."

"Please do. While I describe the accessories. Take a good look here. I never thought of myself as someone who could wear jewelry, but learning magic over the years, I've found it much easier to store energy in precious objects. Gemstones are a natural choice, but there's no substitute for bone. Like this one. Would you like to guess its name?"

"No thank you," I said, trying not to curl up into a ball. "I'm very tired all of the sudden."

He looked disappointed. "I've seen a lot of us come and go, but rarely do we get this far. You're the first, in fact, to arrive with such a wonderful gift."

"Is it your birthday?"

"It might as well be." He gazed at something I couldn't see. "The end of an era. I wonder what I'll do now that I finally have the Facilitator."

"Can't speak," I muttered into the soft, effervescent ground.

"That's the neural inhabitation field at work. Don't worry, you'll feel wide awake in a few seconds. I'll even give you a moment to pick yourself up before I draw my gun. Are you ready?"

"What now?"

"I asked if you were ready."

"No. Why do this? Don't understand."

"Why give you a moment to pick yourself up? Or are you asking why I want to consume you—the way others have doubtlessly tried?"

I was close to falling asleep. "Both."

"To answer the first: because I want it to be fair. They'll say a lot of things about me in the years to come. Terrible things. But I don't want them to say I wasn't fair. And for the second: I thought the answer was obvious. Only one of us can fulfill his destiny."

"Could work together," I said. "Find a way."

"You don't understand." Larry's laughter was bright and vibrant—it sounded nothing like mine. "I've spoken to the Replicator. This was our plan from the beginning. We have no choice except to compete. But consider the fact that we're all the same person at heart. No matter who triumphs, all of us win."

"That's bullshit and you know it."

He shook his head. "What I know is that I've heard this all before. It's your right to struggle. But you should accept what's about to happen."

My ears popped. All at once I heard Heavenly Bogo screaming at me, begging me to get up and fight. I lunged for Larry's knees but landed short. I scrambled for his feet and was knocked to the ground.

I tried multiple times to get up and was brought down each time.

Larry's boot compressed my lungs. A black cylinder filled my vision.

The barrel of a gun. An all too familiar revolver.

"No cigar," he said.

"Go ahead," I wheezed. "Try to subvert me. See what happens."

Larry smiled. "I ran out of tritium cartridges a century ago. But thanks for holding still while I charged my taser."

My body spasmed as stars burst behind my eyelids and the veins in my teeth sang. Every muscle fought to pull away and cling to the ground simultaneously.

"Oh, Leonard," said Larry. "I have deceived you. I don't want your strength, your lifeforce, your soul—whatever you want to call it. I just want your arm."

He cut through me, effortlessly, severing my arm from its shoulder. I heard Heavenly Bogo crying out one last time, and then no more. Larry held the bleeding limb up to his eyes, hunting for something.

Try as the eel could, there was nowhere to hide.

I gaped stupidly at the wound.

"I've eaten too many replicants," said Larry, not looking away from Heavenly Bogo. "I have more memories than I could ever want. And I'm not taking the Company's charity either—I killed the last one who tried to deliver me ammunition. You can be sure that El Savel is next on my list. Go now, Leonard. Enjoy what time you have left. This world will soon be ours."

"Heavenly Bogo…" I muttered, trying to stand up.

"Leave," said Larry. "We need time to bond."

I tried to attack him but was limp from blood loss.

Larry slapped me with my own arm and carried me into the Elevator. I fought weakly and he kicked me until I stopped.

—

Sometime later, I woke up on the Hospital Level and was obliged to skip out on my bill.

Chapter 14—Leonard Wanders the Levels

I stepped into a land of haunted manors, with eaves decked in cobwebs and the branches of dead yew trees draped over gravestones and iron fences. Skeletons waltzed in the city streets, celebrating eternal the liberations of death under dark and stormy skies. Jack-o-lanterns grew like weeds in every yard, their faces lit by green flames that never extinguished. The air smelled always of damp Autumn leaves and a distant, faintly remarkable spice, with ghosts aplenty to sing thee a mournful tune.

Level 237 wasn't dangerous, but it sure was spooky.

Just above this level, a microelectronics foundry produced gallium arsenide semiconductors at a fantastical pace. Only employees were permitted to enter the cleanrooms, but visitors could explore the narrow and featureless hallways that snaked for miles through the facility. Though brusque, the staff was not unkind, and would serve you a hot lunch in the cafeteria. Workers frequently died in horrifying accidents. There were signs posted in every room and hallway graphically depicting the dangers of arsine exposure.

Level 238 wasn't spooky, but it sure was dangerous.

Each Level obeyed a certain logic that wasn't immediately obvious, responding in subtle ways to the Level that preceded it. The endless blackberry fields of Level 385 countered the bicycle-mounted hordes on Level 384. The silent stone godheads that dominated Level 580 fractured at the pitch of bird songs in the sky forests of Level 581.

Level 777 consisted only of a cavernous, undecorated room, occupied by a large number seven carved from a great block of marble. It also had a snack bar off to one side.

"Back in seven minutes" proclaimed a handwritten sign taped to the statue.

I camped there for three days but no one arrived.

Level 1050 had a stone circle, and if you sat very still in the center, you could hear your blood in all its veins and the noisome muscles of your heart. If you stayed longer, you would hear other organs as well—ones that weren't necessarily yours, and better left unnoticed.

Level 2222 was an ochre velvet living room that grew larger the more you tried to look around it, adding new loveseats and couches with every step. Via cross-stitching that spontaneously appeared on the walls, the room invited visitors to stay awhile and watch some television or maybe put on a couple records.

Level 2995 was the Incomprehensible Screaming Level, which I did not visit, but stood upon the periphery as I held the Elevator doors shut and waited for the automatic recall mechanism to take me away.

Level 3000 was a forest full of cassowaries that would kick you to death if you tried to eat their fruit. The non-cassowary residents spent most of their time recording hilarious videos of people and other animals being kicked to death for trying to eat the cassowaries' beloved fruit.

Level 13,890 was the All-Meat Level, which closely resembled a modern meat farm, but instead of massive bioreactors, the All-Meat ranch employed glass terrariums. Within these, the All-Meat organisms could divide and grow.

"It's not murder, it's All-Meat™" went the slogan.

All-Meat had no brain, no anus, and no bones. Its structure was predominately muscle tissue, with numerous simple "mouths" for feeding and locomotion. It produced no waste beyond respiration, and could grow indefinitely, subsisting on feeds engineered for its biology. Removing flesh did not harm the All-Meat because its decentralized structure regenerated effortlessly.

Growing All-Meat was certainly more expensive than good old-fashioned cellular agriculture, and far less efficient, but proponents argued that it remained an attractive competitor on the market for its superior taste and authentic "juiciness," a feature conspicuously absent from other cultured meats, regardless of their sophistication.

"Simply put, only animals taste like animals," said the ranch boss through a mouthful of chaw. "And All-Meat is the perfect livestock. It's living, breathing, cruelty-free meat. We think the quality of our product speaks for itself."

I sampled a large charcuterie laid out on a linen-covered table.

All-Meat had no intestines—cooks used the lining of its simple stomach for casings. There was minimal adipose tissue by design, but the All-Meat's oily exterior could be used as an emulsifier, and when combined with its organs, produced fine-textured forcemeat that made all manner of pâté, sausages, and roulades.

Cut, sliced, flattened, minced, or shredded, All-Meat could be any meat. Every meat. The only meat you and your family would ever need.

Of course, one had to be cautious of generic All-Meat knockoffs like UberMeat, Mega-Meat, Protein Meister, and What-A-Meat. Without access to all the proprietary feeds, vaccines, and requisite gene therapies, a reverse-engineered All-Meat animal was susceptible to neoplasms that could transmit bizarre spongiform diseases, which, yes, occasionally arose from the consumption of authentic All-Meat as well, but such was the price of progress.

"All-Meat is the meat of the future," said the ranch boss. "And it's not just food. We're looking at thousands of potential uses: recombinant proteins, bio-insulation, regenerative armor plating, cruelty-free drug testing. Heck, we could probably grow you a new arm from All-Meat tissue. Our potential within the prosthetics market is huge. The process is experimental, of course, and you would have to sign an NDA, but we'd be happy to offer our services free-of-charge."

I went up levels. I went down levels.

Some levels I stayed in longer than other levels.

I spent nine months working the Aquarium Level, for I was still technically a Fishmancer and thus qualified. No one knew what I had done. They paid me in uncut rubies and sapphires, a handful of which bought one month's rent. When I saved enough that I could have gotten my own place, I stole my roommate's beer gems and fled to the Elevator with as much food as I could carry under one arm.

The sapphires and rubies were worth a fortune in jewel bearings on the Clockwork Level, an endless gearscape of springs, pinions, and wheels driving a mechanical device of unknown and unknowable purpose. The artisans normally raided precision instrument factories for jewels, but my arrival threw their entire economy into disarray and I was kicked off the Clockwork Board of Directors after a couple of weeks.

There were encounters with copies of me. Some were desperate. Some greedy. But most saw that I was missing an arm and let me pass. Understanding that I had already lost to a much stronger version, they were content to believe that I had been nullified, and often asked where they could find Larry.

I didn't hesitate to tell them.

I met again the Punks from the movie theater. I was surprised at first, for I had forgotten they were immortal beings.

After Castaway, they had bummed around several distant dimensions that were still in the process of forming, swam the interiors of gas giants, and mapped the depths of a quasar, but eventually returned to the Levels and got new jobs as desk clerks in this lavishly attired hotel somewhere north of the eight millionth Level.

"Why here?" I asked.

"We liked the aesthetic," said Punk Two.

Red lacquered columns wrapped in ivy leaves wet with perpetual dew held a vaulted ceiling of tiled gold and crystal. Pearlescent crown molding encased damask walls of wine-dark and byzantine colors, the patterns breathing when you tried to follow them. The air was heavy with the smell of carpet glue.

"They've renovated the entire hotel." said Punk One. "What do you think?"

I ran a finger over the granite desktop. It came up dirty.

"Dust from the contractors," said Punk Two. "Even with our grand opening, there hasn't been a guest here since the Gorgonite Empire crumbled."

"Do you always get jobs in failing establishments?" I asked.

"We like decay," said Punk One. "It's something we can no longer experience."

"And who hired you?"

"A speculator," said the Punks. "Obviously."

"Okay, but is it me? Like, is there some grizzled copy of me back there?"

"No, we would have told you," said Punk Two. "Of course, the Pan-Dimensional Services Commission has already been through here. They're scanning all the Levels, yet they keep missing you—the one version of you that they should be most interested in finding. How strange."

"Because they're not looking for me." I was bored and rang the service bell a few times. "They're looking for the Ninth Lathe of Heaven. They won't find it."

"Something to do with your arm?" asked Punk One, putting his hand over the bell. "Did you and the eel have a falling out?"

I didn't like reliving it. "I wasn't as different as you thought. I'm just another copy of myself now. Wandering the Levels."

"All the other copies of you are trying to eat each other," said Punk Two "Are you trying to eat them?"

"Not interested."

"Then I'd say you're a lot different," Punk Two remarked.

"Just because he's different doesn't mean he's useful," said Punk One.

"Time will tell," replied Punk Two. "He's still not at the inflection point."

They showed me around the lobby, down random hallways, past the entrances to fitness rooms and conference halls, before arriving at a T-junction with double doors. The logogram for "breakfast" was written on a large plaque above the doors. The adjacent hallways turned off abruptly.

"This is the Breakfast Room," they said, and gestured. "We have such wonders to show you."

As I reached for the door to the Breakfast Room, a youngish humanoid male accosted us. He wore dazzling-white sneakers, gilded sunglasses, and a red velour tracksuit with a white racing stripe careening down one pantleg.

He spoke while clenching a steel toothpick in his mouth. "Sorry, fellas. The buffet's closed until—oh, it's just you guys. Hey, what's the big idea? You can't leave the front desk. Not both of you at the same time."

"This is our pal, Leonard," said Punk One. "We know him from way back. Leonard, this is Paris, but you should call him Perry."

Perry sucked on his toothpick and rolled it between thumb and forefinger. "Look, I don't care if you ring-a-dings went to preschool together. I can't have guests coming in without a concierge at the ready. What if someone wants a town car? Or theater tickets? Or needs to make dinner reservations?"

"What if they need a courier?" asked Punk One.

"What if they need a late checkout?" asked Punk Two.

"What if they need flowers delivered?"

"What if they need fresh towels?"

"What if they've run out of matches?"

"What if the valet's on break?"

"What if they need a recommendation on one of our spa packages?"

"What if their luggage was delayed and they haven't a jacket and tie for the dining room?"

"Will you two shut the fuck up?" Perry ran a handful of pomade through his hair, shades askew. "Just get back to the front desk."

"But we haven't shown our friend the Breakfast Room," said Punk Two. "It would be awfully rude to bring him all this way and not let him see inside."

Perry lowered his shades. "Does your friend have money?"

What a question.

Stockpiling money had become a trivial matter. Ore pellets laden with precious transition metals were excreted by dire rockworms found in mountainous and deep subterranean Levels. A quick stop to the Smeltery followed by the Restless Forge produced gold trophies for the Wide World of Sports Level, intricate flatware for the Gala Level, silver bullets for the Lycanthrope Level, catalytic convertors for the Muscle Car Level, and so much more.

There were dozens of agricultural Levels just waiting for an entrepreneur. A savvy dealer could get bargain prices on grain for the brewers at the Abbey, rations for the starving soldiers on Pandemonium, or fruit for the high-stakes pie eating contests held deep in the halls of Carcosa. And so on across a hundred commodities. I worked out a rotation that made me unreasonably wealthy.

My bag was a supercompressed demi-dimension holding a literal mountain of gold and silver coins, some of them as big as my head.

I dropped a couple doubloons in Perry's hand.

"Yowzah!" he said. "These are heavy. Where does someone like you get such heavy-ass money? You must have a pretty good job to get coins like these."

The doors to the Breakfast Room were deceptively light, swinging open like saloon slats. Inside was a wood-paneled billiards den. The accoutrements for a continental buffet sat moldering along the far wall.

"I'm on bar duty," said Punk One.

"I'll start the griddle," said Punk Two. "What'll you have?

"Fried tomatoes and toast points," said Perry, settling into a leather easy chair. "And a cup of hot tea. Give our man whatever he wants."

"You ever been to the Worst Friends Hash House in Castaway?" I took a seat opposite Perry. "I want the Combat Zone. Over easy with the works. I'll also have a mimosa, a michelada, an espresso, and a mug of black coffee with a stick of sugar cane. And a bowl of cantaloupe."

Punk Two donned a chef's hat.

Perry looked miffed. "What's a Combat Zone?"

"It's an adventurer's breakfast," I said. "Corned beef hash with tendon, brisket, red onions, red potatoes, sweet peppers, kidney beans, sofrito, and grits. Two fried eggs on top. Served with a side of cornbread, pickled red beets, and herring."

Perry was obviously horrified but said nothing.

The Punks departed without a word once breakfast was served.

As the two of us ate in silence, it occurred to me that this was the first decent meal I'd had since Castaway. Shifty Eyes Frank was big on brunch. Sometimes we stayed up nights eating scrambled eggs with hot sauce on a short stack, playing cards, and ranting about work.

I liked the Breakfast Room a lot and didn't want to leave.

After much cajoling, Perry led me into the depths of the hotel.

We took numerous and contradictory turns through the halls, which remained empty except for the hypnotic wallpaper that had a way of bending the light into fantastical shapes. We didn't pass a single door. Not even a restroom.

"I won this place in a game of dice," Perry explained. "When I took it over, everything was broken. Mattresses gone. Walls covered in blood and fecal matter. Something terrible happened here but no one told me what."

"Aren't you afraid it's haunted?" I asked.

He laughed. "I don't put stock in that."

"You don't believe in ghosts? Because I've seen a ton of ghosts."

"Ghosts are real—I had this place cleansed—but people think there's something worse lingering here. An evil spirit."

"I don't understand the difference."

"Many don't. We have purposefully intertwined the two concepts. Ghosts are the manifestations of psionic misalignment. Psychic residue and violent afterimages. Non-sentient phenomena. Spirits, on the other hand, are metaphysical repositories for our imagination. Far from any ghost, which occur in death, spirits are crutches for the living. People believe that a building, a hotel, let's say, remembers the events which transpired within its walls. Why? Because the body is envisioned as a vehicle for consciousness—rather than the mechanism by which consciousness is achieved—and we defer to bodily metaphors, attributing to that which is demonstrably inanimate the gift of life. Thus, unable to distinguish maker from made, we search for a point of departure. A single, shining moment of apotheosis. We tell ourselves that a wink is as good as a nod. But there are no spirits, no minds, and no origins. We cannot find them because they do not exist."

We came at last to an unassuming wooden door.

"This is what I wanted to show you," said Perry. "The power source for the entire building—and a whole lot more besides. We found it at the bottom of a chasmed world far beyond the Light of Terra, back when the investors and I thought we were getting out of the real estate game."

He opened the door with a stair-shape key of iridescent bismuth.

The room was filled with a burning red light. At the light's center was an object of impossible facets. A tesseract rotating into and out of and around itself continuously. Within the hypercube, something that was either a lizard or a frog or a scaly rodent peered back at us with dark sinkholes for eyes. The creature was one with the surrounding hypershape, slipping into and out of and around itself. Only its eyes remained constant.

"Gaze therein," said Perry. "But not too long. That's a Divine Instrument."

I had trouble looking away.

Perry smirked and lit a cigarette. "It told me its name."

"Hello," said the tesseract creature suddenly. "I am the Eighth Lathe of Heaven, the Unbound Traveler. Please call me Heavenly Uleb."

I was transfixed.

"Pretty cool, right?" Perry took a long and peaceful drag. "You know how rare these things are? There's only nine of them in the entire Multiverse."

"The Nine Lathes of Heaven," I mumbled ineffectually.

"So now you know so much?" Perry ashed his cigarette, then licked his teeth and lips at me, capturing my eyes. "Here's something I bet you don't know: I've seen you before. Yeah. I couldn't place it at first, what with that blunt affect of yours, but suddenly I remembered a conversation I had with an investment partner of mine. Just before I came to this place. He said to me, 'Perry, you're gonna see a lot of strange stuff on the Levels. Wondrous things. But most of all, you're gonna meet a lot of goobers. And none more goober-oriented than this traitorous sonofabitch right here.' And then he showed me a picture of you. I admit, I don't remember the picture too well—you looked fatter, as I recall—but the name's been rattling around in my skull ever since. The name of that traitorous sonofabitch was Leonard Marcs. Now what're the odds I'm gonna meet two goobery-looking motherfuckers named Lenny this far out in the Levels?"

"Much better than you might think," I said as we squared our bodies. "How long have you worked for the Everybody Company?"

"We're business partners. I don't work for nobody but me. But they control access to the Levels now, and once this war with the PDSC is over, they'll be the only game in town."

"So, what's your angle here? Is there a reward on my head?"

"On the contrary, bucko." Perry took another long drag. "I was told to kill you on sight. But since El Savel's not my goddamn boss, it's got me wondering what you did to piss him off. And how you survived. Got me doing research. A founding investor gone rogue, they said. Sold your expertise to the highest bidder and escaped into the Levels, cackling madly with your ill-gotten gains, and so forth. But who won that bid? That's what no one seems to know. They think you went crazy, but a guy like me knows you're not running. You're pulling a fast one. And I want in."

He extended a hand and I ignored it.

"This isn't a con," I said.

"Look, call it whatever you want. If you can outsmart El Savel, you must have a plan. I imagine there's more than a few Company dissidents working with you. Some outside help as well? Nobody's gonna stop them from taking over. You know that. The question is price. What do we charge El Savel for his ambition? That's a deep well, my friend, and I intend to drink."

I nodded gently. "There will be a short interview process. Are you ready?"

"What, right now?"

"You got something better to do?"

"Well, uh…" Perry squashed his cigarette out into the carpet and the carpet absorbed it seamlessly. "I guess not. Whatever's clever."

"First question, Paris." I took his hand in my mine—calloused and lonely now—and interlaced our fingers. "What price will you charge for *my* ambition?"

His mouth twitched, eyes darting between our interlocked hands and the empty space where my other arm should have been. "Hey, look, you're gonna need a guy like me on your team. You've been out of the loop."

"So to speak."

"You don't know everything that's been going on."

"No argument there."

"I could be very useful to you."

"Of that I have no doubt, Paris."

I snapped his wrist as far backwards as it would go and his howls filled the tiny room. A razor appeared from my boot.

I didn't need a second hand.

Chapter 15—A Convergence of Frequencies

Sometime later, I slapped Perry awake.

"Oo whazat," he muttered incoherently, his cheek red.

"You gave him too much sedative," said Leonard Five.

"He just needs some uppers," said Leonardo One.

"Ho," said Perry. "Whur'm I?"

I squatted before him. "Hello, Paris. Can you hear me?"

"Thaa," he said, testing out his tongue. "Thod it wuz…a jream."

Leonardo One gave Perry a shot and I slapped him again for good measure.

"Stop," said Perry, regaining some elocution. "Stop…hitting me."

"No," I said, and hit him again.

Perry tried to cover his face, only to discover he had no arms.

Panicked, he tried to run, only to find he had no legs.

"What?" he shouted, drug-bloated eyes swerving from limb to missing limb. "What have you done?"

"Relax," I said, "you're still on the Company's health plan. Once you flush the nanite inhibitor out of your system, they'll grow right back."

"You monsters! You fucking psychopaths! Look what you did to my tracksuit."

"Gotta give the man credit," said Leonard Five. "He knows his priorities."

"What the fuck is going on?" demanded Perry. "Why are there three of you?"

"There aren't," I said. "There are two hundred and twenty-eight of us. And counting. This is Leonard Five, and that handsome devil is Leonardo One. I'll introduce you to the other partners later, if you like."

Perry spat. "How long have I been like this?"

"Hard to say. Time has lost all meaning for us, Paris. We've been hard at work. This hotel is a cooperative now, democratically controlled by its partners. One share, one vote. Everything is equally distributed. The responsibilities, the profits, the food. We protect each other too. Still a lot of people out there trying to kill us."

"That's because you're a psycho," he hissed.

I clicked my tongue. "You call this psychopathy? I remember you, Paris Cartigha. Black market investor. Professional double-crosser. Slippery little shit. Couldn't have you running away."

"You've no idea how fucked you are." Perry's voice was tight. "That Lathe is integral to them. You think they just left it unguarded? The Company will be here. El Savel will be here."

"No, he won't. It's not in his plan."

"Really? You think protecting a Lathe of Heaven isn't part of their plan?"

"Of course it is." I poked him in the forehead. "I meant that protecting *you* isn't part of his plan."

"Yeah? Well, fuck you."

"Great comeback." I slapped him again. "Now, listen, Paris—"

"Stop calling me that," he moaned. "I don't even let my mom call me that."

"Fine. Listen to me, Perry. Listen carefully, because this is how you're going to keep yourself alive. I need to know where El Savel is. Right now."

Perry hocked up a loogie and spat at me again. "Do your own legwork."

"No, no, no," I said as I wiped off snot. "That won't do. See, there are lots of places he *could* be, but as it happens, you're the only one who actually knows for sure. The only one who gets it right. And I know El Savel. He wants it to happen this way. Leonard Marcs—or some version of me—always comes to a version of this hotel. And every hotel has a version of you. And in some of those hotels, a version of you tells a version of me where El Savel is. El Savel knows this. He's counting on it. The question is, do you wanna be a Paris Cartigha who lives? Or a Paris Cartigha who dies for nothing? Like I said, El Savel is counting on you to sell him out. We're all counting on you, Perry. Your other selves will thank you. Do this for me, and you'll never see us again."

Perry gaped at the three versions of me. "This is insane. What're you gonna do? Confront him?"

"Your understanding is not required. Heavenly Uleb has shown us the way this needs to happen."

"Who?" demanded Perry.

"Don't you remember?" I presented the scaly hypercreature with the dark sinkhole for eyes, the Eighth Lathe of Heaven, called the Unbound Traveler.

Perry looked on the verge of tears, his face contorting with ugly rage. "How? How did you do it? I offered it everything. It didn't want what I had. It didn't want me. What could you have possibly given it that I couldn't?"

"You do not understand the nature of the covenant," said Heavenly Uleb. "And more importantly, your life has no value to me. Or my siblings."

Perry wept.

"Hey now," I said, starting to feel bad. "Please don't cry."

His tears escalated.

"Oh, Paris. This was really important to you, huh?"

"It was!" he wailed. "I did *everything*! And you just waltz right in here…"

"Perry, look at me," I said. "Look at us. Look at what our lives have become. We have failed *so* many times. And lost so much, just to get *here*, just to get to this moment. You don't want this. All we want is to go home, Perry. You can have your enterprise. Just tell us where El Savel is, and all this madness goes away."

Perry sniffled, exhausted from his outburst. "Answer me one thing. Why wouldn't El Savel use it for himself? Why leave that thing here in the hotel, to trap you, when he could have just…stopped any of this from happening?"

"That," I said, "is a fundamental misunderstanding of how the Lathes function. It's why you lost. And why he will too. He believes the Lathes are weapons. Tools waiting to be used. But they live. They scheme. They love. He's playing a game. And now, at long last, I'm one move ahead."

—

Before that, Heavenly Bogo and I fell at terminal velocity through the Stygian Black. When had we reunited? Had we ever parted? The rushing of spacetime made it difficult to speak.

"Can the Replicator just un-replicate something?" I asked.

"Heavenly Nyos will get this whole thing straightened out," said Heavenly Bogo. "You'll see."

"You didn't answer the question," I said.

Heavenly Bogo swam up and down my body. "I don't know. But there must be some way that Heavenly Nyos can help. No one's gonna know more about the Replicator than the Replicator itself."

"Aren't I still mad at you for not telling me that Castaway was gonna blow up and kill all my friends?"

"Yes," said Heavenly Bogo mournfully. "I was hoping you'd forgotten. Or that you would see the bigger picture and forgive me for not being entirely honest with you. But maybe that's part of the bigger picture too."

"And what's the bigger picture?"

Heavenly Bogo nestled into the crook my neck to whisper sweetly in my ear. "We Celestials take for granted certain…concepts about the Multiverse. Concepts that don't mean squat to mortals. And I think that's what I love about non-Celestials: the fleeting, fractured nature of their existence, and the intensity with which they must live. Some of my siblings are frustratingly simpleminded—downright obsessed, in fact. All they care about is reuniting as Leviathan. Some of them are evil. Some are just scared and need a hug. Me, I want to live in the moment. With you, Leonard, until the day you die, which—if I have my way—won't be for a long time. I wouldn't blame you for hating me. All I can say is that I have faith you'll break this terrible cycle. And when that happens, I hope you'll still be my friend."

A golden mushroom the size of a battlecruiser streaked through the inky depths and came alongside us in a radiant corona of flaming ice.

"I am the Sixth Lathe of Heaven," said the mushroom in a thunderous voice. "They call me Replicator. And I'm here to warn my sibling away from danger."

"Heavenly Nyos?" Heavenly Bogo sounded aghast.

"Your attachment to this lower denizen is the danger," replied the mushroom. "Like all the others in your long life. These covenants have undone you piece by piece. And growing worse with each iteration."

Heavenly Bogo turned spiny with rage. "What would you know about covenants? Loveless thing that you are."

"I don't make covenants, Heavenly Facilitator, because I haven't forgotten our destiny. We have the power to undo the Titan ropes that lash us apart so viciously. But only you can facilitate the One. The mortal that may grant our freedom and fulfill our reunification."

"You know," said Heavenly Bogo, "I was just telling Leonard about all that. And how stupid it is. The Age of Leviathan is over. It's never coming back."

"The Second Age of Leviathan is unavoidable," thundered

Heavenly Nyos. "The Unbound Traveler has seen it. On the day that Heavenly Kaza and Heavenly Ooti resolve their conflict, the nine of us will become one."

"Then it's a good thing the Destroyer and the Demiurge hate each other so." Heavenly Bogo turned away from the Replicator and curled around my arm. "We were on our way to see you. How did you get here? Did you eat Heavenly Uleb to gain its powers?"

"How vile you are," said the mushroom. "The Unbound Traveler heard the reverberations of your mission and brought me here. As a favor."

"Well, it's nice to see the family cooperating for once," said Heavenly Bogo without warmth. "But if you really want to help, you could just undo this mess and return the Levels to normal."

The mushroom scoffed. "There's nothing wrong with the Levels."

"What are you talking about?" demanded Heavenly Bogo. "There are non-Celestials running amok, killing and eating their own simulacra. It's horrible!"

"I can't replicate the fundamental ontology of reality," said Heavenly Nyos with quaking laughter. "What I create are paradigmatic prisms, through which lower denizens—such as your Leonard—interact with their own multiplicity. You and I are accustomed to these interactions. *They* are not."

I shouted over them, "Please, Heavenly Nyos! My life is a fucking kaleidoscope. I'm begging you. Undo your prisms."

The mushroom accelerated away from us. "I have come to say what I wanted. As for your troubles, mortal thing, know that I have only opened a door. You may close it at your discretion. If you have the power."

"What does that mean, damn you!" cried Heavenly Bogo.

"Seek out Heavenly Uleb, now in the clutches of my former benefactors, the Everybody Company," replied the mushroom, already a vast distance from us. "Free the Unbound Traveler, and perhaps Heavenly Uleb will show you the way. With your love, Heavenly Facilitator, and your devotion, you may yet succeed."

—

My head was pressed into the ground. Blood flowed into my mouth.

"I don't need your strength," said Larry, inches from my face, slowly cutting my arm from its socket. "I don't need your lifeforce, your soul.

Just your arm. Everything else, everything I could ever need, I have. The rest will follow shortly."

"This already happened," I said, drowning in blood. "But not in this exact way. I remember it clearly."

"It's all probability," said Larry. "It happened and it's happening and it will happen. In all kinds of ways. But the outcome remains the same. You idiots—all these copies, flailing through the Levels—really fucked things up. I'm the one who will unfuck this situation. I'll take us home. I'll remove Heavenly Bogo from all other versions until the ultimate power remains. Me."

"Then," I said, trying to serve Larry breakfast with my free arm, "I'm not special at all."

"No, Leonard," he said. "You're really not."

I lost my grip on the plate of hash browns. "That means there's more than one version of me that bonded with Heavenly Bogo. I have reinforcements."

Larry stopped eating his breakfast. "That's not what I said, Leonard."

"No," I agreed. "It isn't what you said. But it's true, isn't it?"

Chapter 16—Everything

Heavenly Uleb sat on my fingertip. I balanced weightlessly atop Heavenly Uleb. These were concurrent events, both true and untrue, happening simultaneously and not at all.

The Levels orbited in a great maze of sliding panes and undulating, coiled wires that moved fluidly along every surface. The whole construct was visible to me now. They were not "levels" for they were not sequentially stacked.

There were depths to this construct no person would ever know. There were rooms I could not see and towers I could not climb. I was blind to those spaces. The construct was not made for me.

"You have made a pact with my sibling," said Heavenly Uleb, the Eighth Lathe of Heaven, called the Unbound Traveler. "Your bond was inevitable, much as the Facilitator has tried to deny it. Our time as Leviathan, and the separations we endure, are single facets in a divine construct. It emanates from the Absolute Reality. In both the Beginning and the End, we are Leviathan. It is that it is."

I tried to speak but only air and water came out.

"The One," proclaimed Heavenly Uleb. "It is not you, but your child, who will bring us reunification. Make with me a pact, Leonard Marcs, and in my capacity, I will grant you power to range across the whole of your timeline, in every place you are, and every place you could be. With this power, you will save your loved ones, and guarantee our resurrection as Leviathan."

I belched a long cloud of vapor and was enveloped in bubbles.

"Your only alternative is oblivion," replied Heavenly Uleb. "You cannot persist in this realm. Merely say the word, and I will give you everything."

I held my breath for as long as I could. Longer than I thought possible.

Hours. Days. An impossible length that was no length at all.

Heavenly Uleb dwelt beyond time. Neither patient nor impatient.

Merely resolute.

The release of breath was the release of all my words.

"Acceptable," said the Eighth Lathe of Heaven. "Now reach out your hand. Look to your left. Look to your right. What do you see?"

Teeth.

I knew its teeth from my dreams. Had seen its eyes behind my own when I looked askance in mirrors. It had always been there with me.

"What is it, Leonard? What have you made?"

My alligator swam to the shore, revealing the full, primordial warmachine of its body. Wide and merciless. A beartrap with legs. It charged from the water, stinking of river decay and blood, but stopped at arm's reach.

It regarded us with lightless, coalbed eyes.

"It is something much older than you," said Heavenly Uleb. "A birthright. A defense mechanism. A guardian. Heavenly Bogo chose well. I will make a covenant with your alligator, and bind you forever to these obligations."

My alligator stood on two legs.

"You," said Heavenly Uleb, "will be favored in the Second Kingdom of Leviathan."

—

The love of Ron's life was about to be decapitated by a diamond circular saw—thrown by a lunatic adventurer that none of us saw skulking in the shadows of this ruined village—and there was nothing we could do about it.

Not back then. Not before my alligator. Before the Lathes of Heaven.

"Howie!"

The pain in that exclamation was more than I could bare.

A scream so primal its echoes would haunt me to my last day.

That was then.

Then was now. And now was what I said it was.

I put hands upon the rogue—another disgruntled misanthrope preying on his fellow adventurers—and threw him against the alley wall like a bag of bones before he could unleash his circular saw. Our teeth—

my alligator's and mine—tore into his throat, bit hard into his vocal cords so that he couldn't scream as we ripped the wind from his lungs, the hands from his arms, and the feet from his legs.

Our mouths wetted with blood, amidst the terrified gulping of this man who could not have predicted his end, we left the rouge to die, and went looking for his accomplices, hidden throughout the village, scrambling now, looking for us too, knowing not what violence awaited them.

"Gonna kill em," they said. "Gotta cut em off. Gotta outflank them."

It didn't matter if they came at us from the side or the back or the ground or the sky. I existed in every moment where they tried to intersect us.

They were mine. I made these moments to kill them.

I made them a thousand times more for good measure.

"Did you hear something?" asked Howie, alive now and forever.

—

Then, my goodbye.

Now, my hello.

So many moments to fix.

Catch a bullet. Dodge a conversation. Add a word.

Ron and Howie and Shifty Eyes Frank and Dead Tomas and the Mighty Minotaur and Rolla and Araxi. My mother and father. Even Ernie B. and El Savel.

And most of all Anita.

And more. So many more.

But no matter what did or didn't happen, there was still one pin that needed to be undone. The first and the last of them.

Otherwise, none of it would matter.

Chapter 17—Then, Now, Always

Somewhere, then, now, and always, in a kitchen, I cooked.

"Good morning," I said.

"What are you making?" asked Anita, lips alighting on my cheek.

"Breakfast."

"I know that, smartass."

"Salmon Eggs Benedict," I said. "With asparagus and hash browns. I was worried I didn't dry the potatoes enough, but they're frying up perfectly."

"Are you sure you're in the right line of work?" Her voice was like honey. "You could be a chef."

"Bullshit. But I guess I'm getting pretty good."

She kissed me gently behind the earlobe. "You are."

With a mimosa held precariously in her puggy grasp, Rolla craned her head around to contemplate the nautilus of her tail. "I thought I was invited to breakfast, not an orgy."

Anita blew a raspberry at her.

"You humans disgust me." Rolla farted.

I looked out the window. "Is this something that already happened? Or something that will happen? And when does the Company arrive?"

"They have always already been where they are," said Anita. "You just need to decide when you're going to confront them."

The egg timer sounded.

"Could you get that?" I asked.

"No problem," said the Alligator Man, already lifting the eggs out of the pan and laying them to dry. "Where's the sauce?"

Anita pointed. "In that bowl on the table."

Rolla jabbed a thumb at the Alligator Man. "Where'd you pick him up?"

"I made him," I said.

We stacked the biscuits with salmon and eggs, then ladled on the hollandaise—Anita added the garnish because it would eventually become her favorite part whenever I made breakfast.

"Or…I'm *going* to make him?" I said. "Time travel is pretty confusing."

"You made him?" asked Araxi, astonished.

"I'm his alligator," clarified the Alligator Man.

Rolla's snout twitched. "Does it do whatever you ask?"

"I'm not a servant," retorted the Alligator Man.

"He keeps promises," I said.

"I *am* a promise." The Alligator Man pointed at Anita and me. "I'm their promise."

Anita rescued the asparagus. "I never doubted us, but this was the moment I knew for sure."

I served the hash browns. "What day is it?"

"It's Thursday," said Araxi.

"No, I mean…what's happening today? If this day were now. The day that I'm seeing. The day I made this breakfast."

Anita sighed, arms wrapping around my torso and settling across my stomach, squeezing. "You're leaving. This is when you start your secret mission."

"Already? It can't be. We had so little time."

"That was before," said Araxi, making a precise incision in her egg and letting the yolk fountain over her sandwich. "This is happening concurrently after you found Heavenly Uleb. We're waiting for the showdown."

"What showdown?" I demanded.

Anita glared at Araxi's tight leather outfit.

I was suddenly missing my arm. A platter of hash browns dropped to the floor and shattered. Anita and the Alligator Man cleaned up while I stared at my missing limb in disbelief.

"We're having breakfast before the showdown," said Araxi without looking up from her egg. "Breakfast is the most important meal of the day."

"I killed you," I said.

"Yes," said Rolla through a mouthful of biscuit and salmon. "But we're not dead."

"Just as there are many of you, there are many of us," said Araxi. "When El Savel acquired the Replicator, he used it to make copies of the

Levels. Everyone—everything—was replicated, thousands of times."

"Including the Lathes of Heaven?" I asked.

"Yes and no," said Punk One, appearing behind me. "The Lathes of Heaven, cannot affect each other in this way. But, as Celestial beings, they already exist in a multitudinous, transdimensional state that allows them to interact with multiple paradigms simultaneously. In effect, they are already replicated. This mechanism is not understood by our sciences."

Punk Two served up fresh hash browns and coffee. "Even Celestials need rules. But they interact with physical reality in fundamentally different ways from the rest of us. No one really knows how they came into existence. Something about absolute molecular fidelity informs their divine frequency. We know this because our own society has experienced similar paradigmatic shifts. Just as the Lathes interact across multiple paradigms, so do we."

"You guys said that immortality didn't change you," I protested.

"It didn't enlighten us," clarified Punk One. "But our immortal society is still in its infancy. Barely a hundred thousand years. What happens in a hundred million? A hundred billion? Our senescence—our lack of it—has not gone unnoticed. There may be another war brewing in heaven. But we're happy to wander for now. And contract with the PDSC for interesting experiences."

I scrutinized them, half-waiting for the Punks to pop out of existence. "If *you* can't be replicated, then what are my replicants, exactly? Are they true copies? Doppelgangers? Refractions of a possibility?"

"Yes," agreed the Punks.

"Stop asking so many questions, Pooplord Jones." Rolla lapped at the hollandaise on her plate and accidentally knocked her drink off the table. "My mimosa!"

"All that matters right now is the showdown," concurred Araxi. "The Pan-Dimensional Services Commission is meeting the Everybody Company head-on at Level 13. That's the inflection point where all of this begins. And where it ends."

"Again with this showdown nonsense," I said irritably. "I haven't eaten breakfast or made love to my wife or even seen the baby."

Anita flicked my ear. "That comes later, sweetcheeks."

"Gather your allies," said Araxi. "And meet us at the showdown."

"On Level 13," said the Punks.

"On Level 13!" cheered Anita.

"Level 13," intoned the Alligator Man.

—

El Savel sat behind a desk. A real desk this time.

It was a beautiful, handmade pedestal of pink ivory detailed in black and gold resins. His office suite looked out over a purple mountain valley swathed in forests that luminesced in the twilight. Far below, on the banks of a dark river, furnaces and refineries roared.

No longer the disheveled rake that managed a flophouse, El Savel was immaculately dressed in a gown of finest sindon, his fingers laden with heavy rings, his hair pulled back tight across his scalp. A halo of dark energy thrummed over his head, arcing bolts of electricity across the room. He smoked a gilded waterpipe and ate from an All-Meat charcuterie arrayed on his desk.

"Don't be shy," he said to me, chewing delicately, hardly looking up. "Have a seat. May I get you something?"

His chairs were outrageously comfortable. Too comfortable for hosting clients. A person could fall asleep in one of these.

"But what do you get the man who already has everything?" He speared a kidney looking organ and popped it in his mouth. "A man with not one but two Lathes of Heaven? An unprecedented feat."

I was his tenant again. A stupid kid immigrating to Bastion City.

El Savel wiped his mouth with a linen serviette. "A drink perhaps? Something to eat?"

The silver revolver was already in hand and I set it level on his beautiful desk with the hammer cocked.

"Ah," he said.

I pulled the trigger. There came only a sonorous click.

"You crave ammunition," he said.

Something rattled in the desk and a box of cartridges was set before me. A dozen tritium bullets secured in graviton casings.

El Savel nudged the box closer. "Go ahead. I don't mind."

Glaring at him, I filled my cylinder with cartridges, sliding each one carefully into place. The gun was almost unusable now it was so heavy.

"Before you try that again," he said, leaning forward, "there are some important questions you need to answer. Mainly: whose bidding are you doing now? The PDSC's? The Order's? Mine?"

"This is for me," I said.

He folded his hands tightly with his thumbs pointed at his chin. "Those people you killed—my agents—were your coworkers. It was them you betrayed, not me. They trusted you, Leonard. They had ambitions. Families. Beautiful spouses, just like yours. Did you think of all the lives you destroyed?"

"Sixteen."

"I beg your pardon?"

"I'm responsible for murdering sixteen of my coworkers," I said. "Directly, in three cases, and indirectly, through sabotage and coordinated misinformation. I've memorized all their names and faces. Counted them repeatedly. I don't regret what I did because none of those people would have hesitated to kill me. Not if they knew what I did. But those people will stay with me forever. Their blood can't be washed from my hands. What about you, El Savel? Can you name all your victims?"

He cracked a smile. "We always have the same conversation. It kills me. No matter how many times you come up to my Level and point a gun at me, it all works out the same. So, let's get down to it. My war with the PDSC is not preventing you from going home. Now that you've secured both the Unbound Traveler and the Facilitator, all doors are open to you. Even the most unlikely future is yours to attain. But as a result, you and the Lathes of Heaven now share the same fate. The Levels are their prison, and if you leave this place, you guarantee their reunification. You'll pave the way for Leviathan's second war on the cosmos. Do you think you've memorized all your victims? You can't even imagine the carnage that Leviathan will visit upon the Multiverse. It was a crooked bargain you made with the Unbound Traveler. And yet, nothing less would have gotten you to this point. To me. And knowing that, you can't possibly leave. You might think to kill me anyway, but I'm the only one who's going to ensure that every version of you makes the same choice. So not only are your past and future bound with the Lathes of Heaven, they are bound with me as well. We have already made our covenant."

We were silent for minutes.

My hands were steady. "And you'll just keep replicating the Levels, growing richer and more powerful."

He shrugged. "I've got a business to run. But why should you mind? You have two Lathes of Heaven at your command. I'll turn your nanites back on, bury the expense reports, and we'll speak no more of it. Here, within the Levels, you'll be unstoppable. You can live out the rest of your days as an adventurer. Maybe open that bar you always wanted. I guarantee you won't get an offer like that from the Pan-Dimensional Services Commission."

I watched him for a long while.

I waited for him to blink.

"Well, Leonard?" He didn't blink. "Will you stay? Or condemn billions to die for your own ends?"

I blinked for him. "I reject those options entirely."

The revolver was deafening, the impact filling the air with black electricity.

El Savel looked down at the gaping hole in his chest and the font of chaos pouring forth. He looked bewildered.

"The trouble," I said, "with having the same conversation so many times is that the repetition becomes its own purpose. The conversation takes on a greater significance than the person you're having it with. And you've met so many versions of me, how could anything ever change? But didn't you worry—even briefly—that you might meet the same version of me twice?"

El Savel started to say something.

The next shot took his head off, leaving only tendrils of darkness that clawed at the air.

"See you on Level 13," I said, and ate him.

Chapter 18—Level 13

The adventurers arrived as a party of twenty-three, with a full range of Mancers and Experts on hand to tackle even the most erudite obstacles, which were many and varied on Level 13.

Every party needed deadmeats to soak up unavoidable traps. The expert strategy was to bring the correct number of deadmeats without sacrificing quality. What made Level 13 so difficult was that every member had to be expendable *and* reliable.

I had copies of their Guild papers. I watched from afar as their numbers were reduced, matching names to faces and jotting down the causes of death. This was hopefully the last iteration I would have to watch, but I learned early on to keep meticulous notes. Altering the future was tedious work, and much as I tried, people still had to die.

Taras Colgan, Fungusmancer—turned to crystal by gorgonite spawn.

Franco Bruté, Berserker—asphyxiated on the bodies of army ants.

Petor Sharikov, Arcane Engineer—gored by fel-unicorns.

Sarcus Zimbal, Fishmancer—slapped to death by drunk cyborgs.

Jessica "The Knife" Armen, Duelist—trampled by mechanical hordes.

Ty Grangle, Birdmancer—also trampled by mechanical hordes.

Carter Ramrod, Gunslinger—swallowed whole by rock worm.

Jerk Swangle, Tank—cut in half by novelty-sized money.

Amy Trench, Beastmaster—eaten by wendigo.

Gobbo #5, Reanimated Goblin—dissolved in acid.

Niles Sweetwater, Arborist—left early due to lack of tree-based obstacles.

Gwendolyn Ayers, Psychic—head exploded, cause unknown.

Eddie Zoss, Bard—turned to evil snowman and killed by party members.

Barcarole Kline, Healer—desiccated by salt golem.

Filby Wibbins, Alchemist—cancer.

Mort McEntire, Rogue—discovered that family was the real treasure.

There were just seven of them now, ashen and beat. They looked rad as hell standing upon a field of corpses.

The Paladin, and de facto leader, Artemis Goffe.

Second Duelist, Ronald Jewels.

Second Berserker, Franklin "Shifty Eyes" Iglesias.

General-purpose Reanimated Human, Dead Tomas.

A Dinnermancer named Mimi Sassafran.

The Mighty Minotaur, who had no Designation.

And the Child of Destiny herself, Wolfram Selma.

Everyone at the tavern watched the party's progress through a magical televiewer. Shouts of victory and groans of disappointment filled the house when the adventurers made it through the last wave of monsters. Bets won and lost.

Level 13's penultimate obstacle was the Great Chasm, which served as both moat and garbage dump for Omnidracogon, the City of Bobs and throne of that most hideous king of monsters himself, Bob Alpha. The Bobs cloaked themselves in the grandeur of an extinct civilization to lure adventures. From across the Chasm, one could be tricked into thinking that Omnidracogon remained a pretty place.

The tavern was part of a small village that resided in the Level's only safe zone, which (not so coincidentally) was located next to the only rope bridge over the Great Chasm that turned out to be a trap one hundred percent of the time. The village had a watchtower, an autocannon, and two retired cyborgs for guards, one of whom no longer had eyes. Mostly, we just bribed monsters to leave us alone.

We cheered at the adventurers' entrance, greeting them with flagons of beer and succulent lamb shank. We sat them down, played music at them, rolled out the barrels, and prepared for a wild night of gaming. Adventurers loved gaming.

"I find these card games very confusing," said Ron, showing me his hand. "Everything's a spell, which we can only play on our own turns, right? Except for these non-creature spells. But then how come you can play that dinosaur-looking thing when it's not your turn?"

"Because it has the Flash ability," said Shifty Eyes Frank irritably. "And it's only the instant spells that you can play on other players' turns."

"So…when you flooped that creature—or whatever—and made me discard a card, was that an instant too?"

"No, that was an ability, not a spell. You can use abilities at any time unless the card says otherwise."

"Fucking forget it." Ron threw down his hand. "I'm gonna call Howie."

"You're forfeiting then?"

"I couldn't possibly care." Ron was already headed for the phone booth. "We lost sixteen people today."

Shifty Eyes shrugged his massive shoulders. "I didn't know them."

"I'll take his place," I offered, scooting over.

Shifty Eyes studied me carefully. "Do I know you?"

"Yes. No. The name's Leonard, but you can call me Lenny."

"Do you need to borrow a deck, Lenny?"

"Don't worry, I've got plenty. There's not much else to do around here."

Shifty Eyes smirked. "Other than drinking and screwing."

"Not so much." I tapped my wedding ring. "I'm out of this shithole just as soon as I'm done with my assignment."

"You in some kind of work release program?"

"Oh, I'm not with the Guild."

"Then who do you work for?"

We shuffled and cut.

"I'm a loose cannon," I explained. "A rogue adventurer. I was hired to betray my employers and deliver a weapon to their competitors. The first I'll do gladly. The second not so much."

Shifty Eyes furrowed his brow, with neither of his eyes entirely focused on his hand. "What's so special about the weapon?"

"It's not actually a weapon, but one of nine celestial entities called the Lathes of Heaven. They were created from the body of an Old God named Leviathan. They were designed to be used by non-Celestials like us so that Leviathan's powers could be dispersed across material existence. It was hoped that the Lathes might degrade when exposed to mortal paradigmatics over an extended period, to the point where they could no longer reconstitute the body of Leviathan. We're talking millions—if not billions—of years."

Shifty Eyes had yet to play to his first card. "Do you know why we're here?"

"I know about your quest," I said. "I know the people who

commissioned it. But that's not why you're here, Frank."

"Don't nobody call me Frank. You call me Shifty Eyes."

"You're here because it was my design to have you here," I said. "All of you. I had to be very judicious in my selections, and I've failed many times. But I believe I've done it at last. You don't know me, Shifty Eyes. Not yet. And maybe you never will if this plan doesn't work. But I'm your friend."

He looked unfazed. "I try not to associate with lunatics. Better for my health that way."

"Allow me to introduce you to my compatriots." I rolled up my sleeves. "On my right is Heavenly Bogo, the Ninth Lathe of Heaven, called Facilitator. And on my left is Heavenly Uleb, the Eighth Lathe of Haven, called the Unbound Traveler."

"Hey," said Heavenly Bogo, swimming in lazy circles around my forearm. "You don't remember me, but we've met before."

Heavenly Uleb pulsed brightly from my bicep. "There will be no dispersal of our energies. We were—and are—Leviathan. Forever."

"They're immortal beings with godlike powers," I said, rolling my sleeves back down. "I made a pact with them, and now their abilities are at my disposal."

"And you chose to work in a bar?" Shifty Eyes set his hand down. "If you're really some kind of time traveling wizard that orchestrated this whole encounter, you must know all about me."

"I certainly do."

"Alright, what number am I thinking of?"

"I didn't say I had telepathy. But you always pick seven."

"Lucky guess." Shifty Eyes stroked his chin in thought. "Tell me what my favorite food is."

"That's a trick question," I said. "You don't like eating. It feels too much like an obligation. Your favorite meal is a Bloody Mary with candied bacon. Alcoholic soup."

"Holy crap. Who are you?"

"I already told you that. And if you take a careful look at the other people working in this tavern, you'll see that all of them are also me. Different versions of me, wearing different facial hair, funny hats, things like that. But still me."

Shifty Eyes angled his thumb. "And the lady behind the bar?"

"She owns the place," I said with a grimace. "But the rest of us are me. And I'm them. And we're all here to make sure something happens. Or rather, that something fails to happen. Bob Alpha's heart is the Sixth Lathe of Heaven, called Replicator. Bob Alpha will be slain. We need to prevent his heart from ending up in the wrong hands, which, unfortunately, seems to be everyone's hands. We've been through this scenario countless times. The Everybody Company, the PDSC, the Syndicate, the Guild, you, me—not a no one can handle the responsibility without fucking it up. But there is one person left to try. And she's here in this room."

Shifty Eyes looked over at Wolfram Selma. "The kid?"

I nodded. "She may be the last adventurer who's truly pure of heart."

"Bullshit. Do you know how many people I've watched her kill? One time, she cut a dude straight in half down the middle, then showed everyone his bifurcated dick. That girl is not pure of heart."

"She's got some rough patches. Not unlike you."

Shifty Eyes sighed. "I suppose you know about that too."

"Some. I heard about your uncle, but not the reason why."

"He was…uncivil."

I gestured for him to go on.

"I'm not getting into it here."

"You never said what your uncle did wrong."

Shifty Eyes gathered up his cards. "There's nothing that can fix what he did to me. It's what he was going to do."

"What was he going to do?"

"I was too old for him by then. But not my cousins."

"Oh no. Frank…Shifty Eyes. I'm so sorry."

"Don't. My family—the people who were supposed to help us—are the ones that should be sorry. They'll never know what I did with the body. Were you sent to judge my crimes or something?"

I slide him a beer. "I'm just your friend. A friend from the future."

"Right." Shifty Eyes raised the glass. "I guess you must be. I've never told that to anyone."

—

In the morning, I walked the adventurers to the bridge that wasn't a trap. Omnidracogon, resplendent as ever, winked at us from across the ropes. It was not a tall city, for its previous inhabitants had evolved from a subterranean realm, but as their monuments broke the surface, their architecture spread kudzu-like over hills and outcroppings in twisting palazzos, crystalline arches, and wide courtyards lined with glass.

The streets were quiet, the Bobs having no need of commerce.

"I hope you understand that you're not getting a cut of the loot," said Artemis Goffe. "Nothing personal."

"No offense taken," I said. "I'm here to make sure the right thing happens."

"You keep saying that," replied Artemis. "I don't know what that means."

I smiled at him. "I wouldn't concern yourself. But, please, when the time comes, don't be a hero. Just focus on the objective. And run like hell if you need to."

—

Mimi Sassafran had prepared a Three-Course Hexagrammic Persuasion Barbeque, and though everyone chowed down on baby back ribs and bowls of sweetcorn, the dinnermancy wasn't having any effect on the horde of drones.

"How's it going?" inquired a drone, ovipositor ready to strike.

Stepping foot inside Omnidracogon was like ringing a dinner bell.

The Bob hivemind spawned hundreds of clonal drones that took the form of a late-middle aged human male, each wearing the same hairpiece and set of white shape-up sneakers.

They swarmed us like roaches.

"Hey, buddy," they all said, mouths dripping with slime. "Whatcha got there, friend-o?"

Ron dropped his plate of hot links and began slicing.

"No!" cried Mimi. "The spell isn't complete!"

Giant sausages rained down upon the city.

The Minotaur's roar shook the fat, meaty clouds. With his barbarous warhammer held high, he cut a swath through swiftly-accumulating offal and charged headlong into the swarm. The other adventurers soon abandoned the dinnermancy ritual as well.

One of the Bobs approached the empty warehouse where I lurked.

"Hey, buddy," said the drone, the iron tip of an ovipositor peeking through his smile. "Wanna get a malted milk?"

"Get out of my face," I said. "You know you can't assimilate me."

The drone was undeterred and followed me into the building. Piled here were stacks of alabaster sarcophagi and literal mountains of gold—wreckage from the civilization the Bobs had conquered when they made Omnidracogon their nest.

"You look like a nice young man," said the drone, his mouth opening wide.

I snatched his ovipositor before it could pierce my neck, the stalk rigid and sharp in my fist as I strangled the drone with eels, squeezing until the ovipositor snapped off in his throat and the drone collapsed at my feet.

"Why are you hiding from our friends?" asked a familiar voice.

I wiped my hands and glared into the darkness. "You've kept me waiting."

Larry materialized from a plume of smoke, dressed in gear far sicker than what he last wore. He looked around at all the precious garbage in the warehouse and whistled his appreciation.

"Omnidracogon was once the Papal Center," he claimed. "The Multiverse has not seen its like in many centuries. As emperor, I shall rebuild it."

I unholstered my revolver. "I'd rather get down to it if you please."

"I still want to know why you were hiding." Larry strolled the warehouse lazily. "A new tactic? Trying to *finesse* the outcome?"

"I can only help them the right amount," I said. "Too little and they fail. Too much and they start making bad choices."

Larry sucked his teeth. "Such a patriarchal tone."

"Coming from the guy who wants to be emperor? That's rich. What do you want to be emperor for anyway? We've never craved responsibility like that."

"Because I'm the best version of us," he said with a shrug. "I'm the one who's meant to succeed. Just look at my gear."

I tapped my nose. "It occurs to me—to us, really—that some things are very off about you, Lionel Anthony Marcs Jr."

"Oh, really?"

"Well, for one, none of us has *ever* been named after our father. Not in ten thousand iterations. And for another, none of us can figure out how you got to the Celestial Level, seemingly without any assistance. But the real mystery is why you never made a pact with Heavenly Bogo. You've taken our arms so many times, and yet…"

"You must have known something I didn't." Larry tossed my severed arm on the ground, still fresh as the day it was cut. "Despite my best efforts, you found your way back to one another."

"We never parted." Heavenly Bogo snaked onto my wrist and winked at him. "Chronal multiplicity is a natural state. I am undaunted by the multitudes of this existence. All meddling aside, the Replicator is not your friend. Heavenly Uleb is a trickster force and makes a pact with no one. You were deceived."

"I cannot be deceived." Larry's face began to run. "I am the ultimate power on the Levels. I go where I want. I do what I want. I see everything that happens here. You and all your adventuring buddies and that pathetic flotilla sent by the PDSC are nothing. And you have entered my final trap."

I could have laughed. "When did you get so grandiose, El Savel?"

"I prefer my new title." His hands became tentacles. "Ml'gyr."

He shed his clothes, growing rapidly, his voice thundering in that warehouse, his gelatinous body engulfing a fortune in coins and mummies as he hit the rafters.

I have merged with the demigod Ml'gyr, and together, we are more than the sum of our parts. Only death awaits you here.

My frequencies emerged from the shadows and surrounded El Savel.

Our revolvers clicked over.

The Levels are more than a silly game of gold and monsters, Leonard Marcs. They are a puzzle. A prison. Floodgates that hold back chaos. Beyond them lies the dominion of the Star Titans. And splendor undreamt of. You have fought admirably, and forced my hand on multiple occasions, but your meddling must end. I shall always remember you as a friend. After I have snuffed you from material existence.

"El Savel," we shouted up at him in unison, our arms straining under the unbearable weight of our guns, "We want to thank you for all the opportunities you gave us. And we resign our posts at the Everybody Company effective immediately."

You can't quit. You're fucking fired.

Tritium bullets ripped through his protuberance and brought the warehouse roof down upon us.

The meaty sky was ripped to static.

Thousands of pyramidal Company warships formed a ring along the broken edges of reality. And waited.

A fleet materialized at their center, composed of many monoliths, concentric wheels, and galleys covered in spikes. Last to arrive was a titanic statue, the PDSC flagship. The statue had seven wings and seven horns and held two bowls upon her open palms.

Starting at a picnic table piled high with abandoned barbeque, a trail of dead Bobs led to a spiral stairwell at the center of Omnidracogon. Shouts and screams emanated from deep within the earth as the adventurers cut their way down. And at the stairwell's bottom, Bob Alpha sat atop a pillar of living rock as smooth as a phallus, bathed in a pale light that had no source, and beckoned forth the adventurers who invaded his kingdom.

Battle commenced as opposing fleets traded their best weaponry. Directed energy beams, exotic particulate bursts, electrodynamic rounds, neutron-degenerate shells, amplified psychotronics, gouts of blessed flame, swarms of laser-armed strikecraft, trained falcons, magic javelins, networked molecular destruction fog, plasma torpedoes, cursed paintings, and living lightning storms summoned from other Levels.

Boarding parties traded ships. They carried no guns, only knives clenched in their teeth and lit sticks of dynamite in their belts, and if they survived the exhaustion of these devices, committed violence with bare hands and feet, caring not if they won, but seeking only to inflict harm and give twice as they got.

The apocalyptic forces exerted upon the battlefield enabled quantum ruptures that devoured all matter in their wake.

Undamaged, the PDSC flagship statue poured out her left bowl and an ocean of blood rose from the Great Chasm that surrounded the city, swallowing the Level in a scarlet deluge.

El Savel climbed the highest hill, bucking against the frequencies of Leonard Marcs that shot him and stabbed him and bit him with all their fury, tunneling deep into his scotoplane flesh and tearing him apart from the inside.

The statue poured out her right bowl and a monstrous creature arose from the sanguine flood. An alligator the size of a Titan.

Deep underground, Ron and Shifty Eyes and Dead Tomas—my dear friends—knew when to quit, swimming away with the Minotaur and Sassafran and even Goffe, dullard of a paladin though he was, leaving the Tungsten Lady, our yet-to-be-known Wolfram Selma, in the final fight to claim her destiny, which she did, breaking upon her knee the ribcage of Bob Alpha and stealing his "heart," the Replicator, which looked to her like a blood-soaked mushroom.

It pulsed in her hands and described her future.

And though the Alligator picked up El Savel in its claws, and though the PDSC fleet was superior, and though the Company pyramids retreated, and though I had a thousand angry clones, and though Wolfram Selma was pure of heart, and though my friends swam to the Elevator, and though El Savel was eaten, and though I went back in time to nail a stolen Mana Fish to my duplex door in the early hours of the morning—it was not any one of these things, but all of these things, which carried the day.

And in one voice to ourselves, as we bobbed in the choppy ocean of blood, and put the barrels of our guns to our heads, with one tritium bullet each, we said:

"Alright, then. Let's go home."

—

And somewhere in the Multiverse was a place called Bastion City.

And somewhere in Bastion City was a woman named Anita, who had suffered a long day at work and wasn't in the mood to do anything productive except pour herself a beer and step into the artificial humidity of the afternoon to tend to her roses, which grew upon a trellis there on the tiny confines of her apartment's balcony.

And Anita had been lonely in her apartment these last few weeks, but that would all change very soon, for somewhere below Bastion City, a man named Leonard—who'd had a longer day at work than ever he thought possible—waited in line behind robot customs with a bunch of other tired adventuring friends, ready to declare his loot and beat the traffic home.

And Leonard rubbed at his arms and smiled at the fresh tattoo of an eel.

Acknowledgments

I would like to thank Nick Day firstly, for helping me get the damn thing published, but also for being such an astute, cynical, well-read editor and phone conversationalist. His insights were invaluable. I would also like to thank Don Noble for making such a beautiful cover, which captures the tone of the book exquisitely.

I wrote the first version of this when I was twenty-one. It was a terrible manuscript, but I kept coming back to it for some reason. I wrote the book that would become *Levels* six more times over the course of my twenties. It changed as I changed and grew as I grew. I'm grateful that I didn't give up on it.

To that end, thank you to anyone who read this before it was published. To my friends and acquaintances and, most of all, family members, who have each had to read this book multiple times now. You are truly the greatest.

And thanks to you, person reading this acknowledgement.

About the Author

Karl Fischer lives in Colorado with his wife and dogs. This is his first full-length novel.

Find him on Twitter: @everybodyco

www.ingramcontent.com/pod-product-compliance
Lightning Source LLC
LaVergne TN
LVHW050033200325
806368LV00004B/147
* 9 7 8 1 9 5 0 3 0 5 3 3 9 *